P9-CKT-051

THE ALAMO TRAIL

THE ALAMO TRAIL

•

Kent Conwell

AVALON BOOKS
NEW YORK

Library of Congress Catalog Card Number: 99-091314
ISBN 0-8034-9401-7

Published by Thomas Bouregy & Co., Inc.
401 Lafayette Street, New York, NY 10003

PRINTED IN THE UNITED STATES OF AMERICA
ON ACID-FREE PAPER
BY HADDON CRAFTSMEN, BLOOMSBURG, PENNSYLVANIA

To all those brave and daring Texans
who dared to dream of a republic
where men could be free.
And to Gayle, my wife, who has
the patience of Job with me.

Chapter One

At the small village of Liberty down in the East Texas Piney Woods, the old-timers had a saying: *When you find yourself in a hole, stop digging.* I reckon that's sound advice, but my luck has always been that sometimes I'd keep digging even when I was trying to stop.

Seemed like every time I opened the front door, trouble was standing there with a big grin waiting to come in. And that's how I came to be curled in my poncho in the mud under a vine-covered windfall with over a hundred blazing fires surrounding me. And crouched around those fires were a thousand of Santa Anna's crack Veracruz and Iguala Regiments, the elite of his army plus a couple hundred vaqueros that tended the animals and drove the pack mules.

I was in this predicament because of one smart move and one dumb move. The smart move was sending Robert McAnella back to Sam Houston with word of Fannin's capture. The dumb move was me acting as a decoy so Robert could escape. Luckily, I'd managed to give the Santanistas the slip, but unluckily, I ended up right in the middle of the entire Mexican army.

Come morning, they'd spot me for sure, and I'd end up a prisoner back at Goliad with Colonel James Fannin. I took a quick assessment of my gear. Not much. A replica of Jim Bowie's famous knife, a pair of ball-and-cap Kentucky pistols in my belt, a Long Tom rifle in my hand, and a fierce determination to avenge the death at the Alamo of my brother, George. And the best way I could do that was to join up with General Sam Houston and take a hand in whipping up on Santa Anna.

The aroma of broiling meat wafted through the chilly night air. My stomach growled, and I ducked lower, hoping no one had heard it. It would be a kick in the head if a growling stomach took away my one chance to escape.

All I could do was wait until they slept, then saunter through the bivouac just as if I was another vaquero. If I kept my head down and stayed away from the fires, I might just make it. If I didn't, if they spotted me, then I'd have my own little Texas revolution right here.

Time passed quickly, too quickly. Voices faded, laughter died out, and finally the camp slept, enveloped by a thick cloud of wood smoke hanging like the night fog a few feet above the ground. Sentries slumped against the rough bark of the live oak or squatted among the wild huckleberries, their eyes fighting a losing battle against sleep.

I had studied the camp carefully and located the remuda. I needed a pony, but only if I could get one without disturbing the camp. I much preferred that the Santanistas remain completely unaware of my presence, even after I was gone.

For the last several days, the weather had been blustery with cold rain and drizzle. Earlier in the day, the weather let up. Now the camp slept soundly.

Silently, I eased to my feet, tugged my slouch hat over my eyes, and shuffled past the dying fires toward the darkness beyond the camp. Under my poncho, I shifted my Long Tom to my left hand and pulled out my knife.

I had less than a hundred yards to the perimeter of the bivouac. With each step, I expected a shout of restraint, of alarm, but the camp slept quietly. From the darkness beyond, I heard the gentle nickers of feeding horses.

The ground was muddy. The slush sucked at my feet, making faint popping sounds with each step. Once, I almost walked over a sentry who had squatted against a large oak and had fallen asleep. My brogan grazed his foot.

He stirred.

I clenched my bowie tighter, but the sentry sighed gently and began snoring again.

My hopes began to rise when I made out the dark mass of the remuda. The animals were calm, and apparently my smell was no different than that of the Santanistas.

A sharp command from the darkness halted me. "*Detenga! Quien es?* Halt. Who is there?"

A darker shadow ghosted from the shadows of the remuda. I gripped the bowie knife tighter and replied in my best Spanish. "*Es Miguel. Usted me conoce.* You know me." I eased my hand from under the poncho. When I struck, I had to be fast and sure.

"*Miguel? Que—*"

I swung the bowie, slamming the butt into the sentry's temple. He slumped to the ground with only a faint groan. I grimaced. So much for the Santanistas being unaware of my presence. I hurried to the remuda.

In the flickering light of the dying campfires, I saw that the vaqueros had strung several ropes in parallel rows to which they tied the horses. Stealing one would be simple. Just wait until the sentry was at the other end of the row, cut the tie-down, and lead the horse into the night.

And cross my fingers that no one spotted us.

I paused at the first line of ponies and studied the night around me. My hopes surged. No sentries. Quickly, I slashed a tie-rope and eased my fingers around the bridle, taking care to press my hand against the nervous animal's muzzle. The feel of human hands calmed the horse. Taking a deep breath, I headed for the complete darkness beyond the firelight.

The night was like pitch. Remaining on foot and keeping one hand extended against the dark, I headed east, keeping the north wind on my left cheek.

We made slow progress. During the night, the slow rains came again. Grumbling, my shoulders hunched, my head down, I sloshed through the mud, stumbling through undergrowth, almost banging into trees. Once or twice I muttered a prayer, wondering if the morning would ever come.

It did, and as soon as the gray dawn began pushing the night away so I could see, I swung onto the large animal and turned north, heading for Gonzales, Sam Houston, and the Texas army.

Without warning a few minutes later, the boom of a rifle broke the morning silence. My pony squealed, lurched sideways, stumbled, and then caught her feet.

I jerked around and spotted six of those red-jacketed Santanista dragoons from the Delores Cavalry spurring their animals toward me. Out of the corner of my eye, I spotted a red furrow across the croup of my horse. Another couple of inches lower, and I would have found myself on foot.

Whipping my pony around, I crashed through a canebrake on my right and burst onto the prairie beyond. Leaning low over the warhorse's neck, I wished for my own little mustang. With him, no one would catch me.

It took a few minutes, but I evaded the patrol.

The drizzle continued, turning the prairie into a foot-sucking mudhole. I slowed the pony into a walking two-step, a mile-eating gait that wouldn't jolt a man's insides to jelly.

The countryside was rolling, a mixture of sprawling prairies intersected by thick bands of scrub and mesquite. I made a point of staying close to the tree lines so I could duck inside if I spotted any Santanistas.

I'd made close to fifteen miles when I spied a Mexican patrol emerge from a line of oak across the prairie to the northwest. Without hesitation, I reined into the thick undergrowth on my right and waited. They seemed to be heading directly for me, so I turned east, toward Coleto Creek, where, I would later learn, Fannin had surrendered.

The mist grew heavier, and the water-filled clouds brought an early dusk as I rode into a patch of willows along the creek, which was slowly rising in its banks. The undergrowth was so thick, a jasper wouldn't have been able to spot a herd of cattle ten feet away.

I rode along the creek bank until I discovered a drift log. I stashed my powder, lead, and weapons in the root ball, hoping to keep my gear dry. The creek was twenty yards wide at this point, so I tied the warhorse to a willow and waded into the current, pushing the log ahead of me. Moments later, I climbed ashore, stacked my gear on the bank, and swam back for my pony.

After crossing back over, I grabbed my gear, clambered up the steep bank leading the horse, and froze at the clink of metal against metal. Slowly, I peered into the thick undergrowth of berry briars and new willow, straining my ears, but all I could hear was the feathery rustle of drizzle on the leaves. A chill swept over me.

Moving carefully, I turned east, leading my pony away from the creek. Abruptly, I pushed through the undergrowth into a clearing, and looked down the muzzle of a .45 Kentucky long rifle.

"Just stop yourself right there, mister," said a white-haired old black man as he held the rifle centered on my chest.

Chapter Two

The clearing was thirty feet wide. The old man stood in the middle. Behind him were five frightened and rain-soaked girls in front of a short haul wagon with a broken rear axle. A double yoke of oxen stood motionless, their hides shiny with rain.

I didn't move. "Just take it easy with that rifle, boy. You've got no trouble with me."

He stood a little straighter. "I ain't no boy, mister. I'm a free man."

One of the girls stepped up beside him. She wore a shawl over her head, and the hem of her blue gingham dress was caked with mud. When she spoke, I saw she was not a girl, but a young woman. "Be careful, Uncle Ned. We don't know but this jasper might be a bandit."

Uncle Ned held the rifle steady. "That's right, mister. You a Santa Anna man?"

I grinned, hoping to put him at ease. "No, sir. Me and a friend was carrying a message from Sam Houston to Fannin. Now I'm trying to get back to the general so we can fight Santa Anna." I glanced around the small group. "Where are the others? Your families?"

The young woman shook her head. "We don't know. All our folks were at a house raising when the rider came with word of the Alamo. We grabbed what we could and left in the middle of dinner. We didn't have time to wait for them, the rider said."

Uncle Ned kept the rifle on me. I nodded to him and spoke to her. "Can you tell him he can put the rifle down now? I ain't going to hurt anyone."

She gave me a sly grin. "No, I don't reckon you will."

Without being told, Uncle Ned lowered the rifle. "We got a busted wagon, mister. Can you help us fix it?" He held up his left hand, frozen forever in a knot of gnarled and twisted fingers. "I ain't much good with this club hand."

I cast a worried glance north. I figured General Sam was some distance from Gonzales by now. And Robert McAnella should be arriving there anytime with the news of Fannin. I remembered my brother, and a fierce hatred flowed through my veins. I sure didn't want to miss out on any of the fighting. I had a mighty big score to settle with Santa Anna, but I couldn't ride off and leave these folks in a bind, not with two thousand Santanistas behind them.

"Let me take a look at the wagon," I replied, tying my pony to a willow. Night was fast approaching, but despite the shadows beneath the wagon, one glance told me the axle was beyond repair.

I looked around at Uncle Ned. "Got any tools?"

The young woman clutched the shawl just below her chin, keeping it tight over her head. "Pa left a few in the wagon. This is his wood wagon that he hauled firewood in."

Tying my horse to a nearby willow, I rummaged through the hastily gathered gear in the wagon bed. A grin popped on my face when I spotted a bow saw, exactly what I needed for the job at hand.

"Look, Miss . . ." I hesitated.

"Kate," she replied. "Kate Rusk." She gestured to the others. "You met Uncle Ned, and this here is Mary Rusk, my little sister. The others are Susanna Zuber, Dilue Harris, and Jenny Adkins. They were spending the day with Mary, and I was looking after them."

I nodded to the group, none of whom looked to be over twelve. I noticed the one named Jenny wore her hair in braids. She appeared to have been crying. One of the girls, a towhead, cradled a rag doll in her arms. They were all bundled and draped in homemade quilts. "Glad to meet you folks. My name's Bob Walker." I glanced at the darkening sky from which a heavier sprinkle had begun to fall. "There's no time to build another axle, though from the looks of the tools in your pa's wagon, Miss Kate, it could be done. I figure the smartest thing to do is chop off the back of the wagon." I indicated the toolbox. "We'll tie the toolbox on the back of the tongue. That'll help balance the weight on the shortened bed."

Kate looked up at Uncle Ned, who nodded agreement. "Fine," she replied. "How long will it take?"

I eyed the four-foot-wide bed. "Not long. An hour, maybe two."

She looked over her shoulder into the deepening night. "You think any of Santa Anna's soldiers are around?"

Chewing on my lip, I peered into the growing dusk, remembering the patrol I'd seen earlier. Had they made camp somewhere along the creek, or had they continued their mission? "Hard to say. I saw some a few hours back. But I don't reckon any of them will be out prowling around. I imagine they're trying to stay dry and warm."

Uncle Ned handed Kate the rifle. "Here, Miss Kate. I'll help the gentleman."

With a brief nod, she turned to the girls. "All right, girls. Let's string the tarps against the rain. Then we'll build a small fire to warm ourselves."

"Make sure it's a small one," I said, cautioning her.

She shot me a cold look. Her reply was even colder. "Don't worry, Mr. Walker. I know what I'm doing."

Taken aback by her chilly response, I started to apologize, but then thought better of it. Why should I? I was concerned for my own neck as well as theirs. I turned to the wagon.

Despite the intensifying rain, Uncle Ned and me had the wagon cut in two, the tailgate wired on, and the oxen staked out for the night in less than two hours. In the meantime, Kate and the girls had rigged a three-sided shelter in which a small fire blazed brightly. Chunks of fat pork sizzled on spits stuck in the ground around the fire.

In the rear of the shelter, the girls had spread a thick layer of grass to keep their quilts off the muddy ground. I couldn't help noticing they'd spread an equal layer of thick grass across along a second wall. For me and Ned, I guessed. In other circumstances, such a snug little camp would have been downright enjoyable.

Kate indicated the grass. "You can throw your gear over there, Mr. Walker." With her scarf removed, I noticed her hair had a reddish tinge, like a strawberry bay, and she'd brushed it as had the other girls.

I nodded, surprised at the civility in her cool voice. I wasn't sure if she gotten over whatever burr I'd put under her saddle or not, but at least her words didn't freeze my blood. "Thanks." I held out my arms. "You're looking at all the gear I have."

Taking off my slouch hat, I shucked my poncho and spread it on the grass, then laid out my rifle and pistols, planning on checking the loads. I could feel five sets of eyes on my back, but I took my time recharging my weapons. I'd had a rifle misfire once when a bear charged me over on the Sabine River. All that saved me was that the old bruin wasn't willing to swim out in the river after me. Since then, I'd always been mighty careful about my pistols and rifles.

One of the girls, Susanna Zuber, scooted around so she could watch me. She looked to be twelve or so, not that I'm any judge of age. And she was curious as a kitten, asking question after question, especially about the pistols.

"Susanna, you stop bothering Mr. Walker," chided Kate.

"She's no bother," I replied. And she wasn't.

She asked, and I explained how pistols worked, pointed out the percussion tube through which the powder was ignited, and demonstrated loading the weapon. She seemed a bright young girl.

Finally I finished. Reluctantly, Susanna retired to the rear of the tent with the other girls. Miss Kate nodded to the fire. "Help yourself. We've eaten."

Slipping out of the Satillo blanket I wore under the poncho, I grabbed a spit of hot pork and a chunk of cold cornbread, and I sat back on the blanket. It was the first time I'd relaxed since I'd reached Peach Creek and General Sam had sent me to Fannin four days earlier.

I'd no more taken a bite than Kate spoke up. "You come from Sam Houston, you say?"

I gulped the chunk of pork and remembered my brother, George. My voice grew soft. "Yep. He sent me and Robert McAnella to Fannin, but by the time we got there, the Mexican army had Colonel Fannin captured and was marching him into the fort. That's when they spotted us. Once Robert and me made the woods, I sent him north to Houston with word of what had happened to Fannin while I led the Santanistas on a fare-thee-well chase. I'd given them the dodge when I found you folks." I shook my head slowly, still thinking of my brother, George.

She looked at me curiously. "Are you all right?"

Her question shocked me from my reverie. "Huh? Oh, yeah. Sorry. You see, my brother died at the Alamo. That's the reason I've got to get back and join in the fight. I've got to make up for George."

The young woman's eyes grew soft and warm. She nodded her understanding. I pushed my own troubles aside and tore off another hunk of pork. "What about you?"

She glanced at the girls, who were all dressed in similar homespun sack dresses, their everyday garments. "Our families live along the San Antonio River." She smiled sadly at the towheaded girl who still clutched her rag doll. "This is Dilue Harris. Her pa was building a new cabin, so all our folks went over to help." The young woman hesitated. I saw the fear in her eyes for her own parents. She drew a deep breath and continued. "The girls stayed with me and Mary. We were in the middle of noon dinner when Uncle Ned got word about the Alamo."

The girl in braids sniffled and rubbed her eyes. Kate shot me a glance as she hugged the girl to her. "Jenny's brother was visiting us, but he was off hunting when we had to leave," she explained. "We couldn't find him. Uncle Ned looked for hours and then caught up with us. Maybe Pa found him when he went by our place."

"You think your pa will? I mean, go by your house."

"Oh, yes." She nodded emphatically. "He and Ma will go by. They'll see us gone, and follow. They won't be all that worried because they know Uncle Ned's with us."

She reached out a slender hand and laid it on Ned's worn wool coat. "We were lucky Uncle Ned was around." She squeezed his arm. "Of course, Uncle Ned is always there when we need him."

I looked at Ned, whose dark eyes were staring deep into the small fire. "He lives nearby, huh?"

Kate shook her head. "Oh, no. He lives with us. He has his own little cabin out back. My grandfather owned Uncle Ned back in Alabama. On the way to Texas, according to Grandpa, the wagon was swept away crossing the Sabine River and Uncle Ned saved my pa, who was just a baby. Grandpa was so grateful, he wrote Uncle Ned a letter making him a free man. Since then, he stayed with us, part of the family."

She kept talking, but the combination of no sleep, grub in my belly, and a warm fire started me nodding off. My head snapped back, and the girls snickered.

I jerked awake, blinked once or twice, and shook my head. "Sorry, ladies," I muttered, rising to my feet. "Didn't mean to doze off."

Kate stayed me. "Sit back down, Mr. Walker. Finish supper. We're all tired. We all need some sleep. Uncle Ned will watch after us."

The older gentleman nodded. "Yessir, Mr. Walker. You get some rest. I'll be looking after you all."

Nodding, I took another bite of pork and cornbread, washed it down with a long drink of sweet water, and curled up on my poncho. The patter of rain on the tarp, the warmth of the small fire, and food in my belly was too much of a combination to fight. Just before I drifted off, my last thought was that come morning, I'd see the small party off toward the Sabine, and then I'd find General Sam and join his army.

Chapter Three

A few days earlier in Fort Bend County, I'd been helping some neighbors on the Brazos River nail freshly split shingles on their house when a courier came galloping down the quagmire we called a road, his pony splashing buckets of mud with every step.

He carried a dispatch stating that Colonel William Travis needed help at the Alamo. "Yessir," he said, spitting out the words faster than the copycat chatter of a mockingbird. "Colonel John Bird is building a company of soldiers up the river at San Felipe. They're pulling out for the Alamo at midnight."

He didn't have to speak twice. We'd been reading all about the trouble with Mexico in *The Telegraph and Texas Register* newspaper that Gail Borden printed up in San Felipe. I'd stopped off here at our old friends', the McAnellas, on my way to the Alamo to join up with my brother, George. We were out of Liberty, Texas.

We dropped our hammers and grabbed up our gear. Robert McAnella and his brother, Pleasant, Merideth Tunget, and me got our horses, extra homespun clothes, our percussion-lock Long Tom rifles, braces of pistols in .35 to .55 caliber, and some grub, and headed out. We had thirty miles of thick mud to plod through. If I'd been by myself, I could have reached San Felipe by nine o'clock. My pony was a small, wiry mustang, with more heart and staying power than I'd ever seen in a cayuse. The two of us were a matched set.

Hours later, at midnight, thirty-two of us Texicans pulled out of San Felipe for the Alamo just as another drenching thunderstorm hit, bringing with it another cold snap. "I ain't never seen a springtime as wet as this one," growled Colonel Bird. "It wouldn't surprise me none to see a fish riding in the saddle next to me."

We rode hard, and the muddy soil made it tougher. The next evening, we reached the Lavaca River and took a short rest before making a sustained run into the Alamo. I led my pony into the river for a drink. I knelt and washed my face, staring at the reflection looking back at me, a skinny drink of water with sun-bleached hair in dire need of a clipping. I never paid much attention to looks, but I guessed I was what folks called ugly. Like I'd fallen out of an ugly tree and hit every branch on the way down.

In the middle of our meal, another courier skidded to a halt. He gave us the bad news that the Alamo had fallen, then in the next breath before he rode on out, he added that General Houston wanted all Texans to meet him at Peach Creek, beneath the big oak on the D. B. McClure plantation outside of Gonzales, several miles to the west of us.

My ears rang in disbelief. All had died. I stared after the courier. I couldn't believe it. Not George, not my brother! I closed my eyes, sick to my stomach.

Around me, men cursed and shouted. We all had family and friends and neighbors there, but now we were more than ever determined to make Santa Anna pay for the massacre. And with grim determination, we set out, knowing the first step in our revenge was to reach General Houston.

And we did, arriving mid-morning the next day. We were ready for a bear-clawing fight.

General Sam stood in the middle of a large crowd of homespun volunteers under the huge oak to ward off some of the drizzle. He was bellowing and waving his arms, about what, we couldn't tell until we pulled up on the outskirts of the cluster of men. I tugged my slouch hat tighter on my head and hunched over so the rain ran down my poncho instead of my neck.

It seems that Fannin had refused to leave Goliad when Houston ordered him out, and Houston was furious. His face was red, his eyes blazed, and his speech was one curse after another. He talked about the Texans whipping up on General Cos in San Antone back in December.

And then he said something that made my heart just hop up into my throat and tears fill my eyes. In his deep, resonant voice, he boomed, "On March the second, just nine days ago, the members of the Convention of 1836 signed the Texas Declaration of Independence, and an interim government has been formed."

A declaration of independence. I remembered my own grandpa rocking on the porch in the dusky evenings dotted with hundreds of little green fireflies and talking about the United States Declaration of Independence, and how it made men free. And now, we were doing the same thing in Texas. Making men free. In his next breath, Houston launched into another harangue on Santa Anna.

Houston spotted us and stopped his tirade in the middle of one of his most colorful invectives. His eyes fixed on my pony. Abruptly, he waved me forward. "Make room, boys," he bawled. "Let the man through."

Still in the saddle, I pulled up in front of Sam Houston. He was tall, his eyes level with mine. Like I said, my mustang was small, a little over fifteen hands, about sixty inches.

Drops of rain glistened on Houston's muttonchop

whiskers, and the fire of Hades burned in his eyes. He laid a big, gnarled hand on the neck of my pony. "I lived with the Cherokee long enough to recognize a fine-looking animal, son. Kinda on the small side."

"Yessir, General. But I'll match him against any full blood you want."

"What's his name?"

"Horse."

He chuckled and looked at me. "What's your name?"

"Robert Jefferson Walker, General. But they call me Bob."

His eyes grew fierce. "How far you come to get here, Bob Walker?"

I shrugged. "A piece. Hundred miles or so."

He patted my mustang's neck. "Think Horse there can go another sixty or seventy?"

"General, I had a brother at the Alamo. Me and Horse here can go a thousand if we got to."

His face darkened with anger, and then a faint smile curled one side of his lips. "Just sixty or seventy, son. That's all. You got a friend with a pony that could go that distance with you?"

My eyes fixed on his, I replied. "Yessir, General. Robert McAnella yonder. Me and him have been racing for years. 'Course, I always got the best of him."

Houston laughed and waved Robert to him. "Come here, boy."

Robert pulled up beside me.

Houston eyed the Long Tom lying across Robert's saddle. He nodded to my saddlebags. "You got plenty powder and lead?"

"Yessir." I patted my saddlebags. "We got us enough to start a war of our own."

He exploded with a curse. "Then you boys hightail it for Goliad. You tell Fannin if he doesn't get over to Victoria and set up a perimeter of defense, when I get hold of him, I'll kick him all the way to Washington-on-the-Brazos. You hear me, boys?"

"Yessir," we answered in unison.

"And keep a keen eye out for Comanche. Word is they're taking advantage of our fight to steal what they can." He paused, then added, "And you boys hurry back. I can't afford to lose good men like you, you hear?"

Robert and me nodded in unison. After a few fast good-byes, we were off.

The steady drizzle carried a chill, but I never felt it because of the fury flogging away at my nerves. Several times during the seventy-mile ride, we came across Texan families in heavily loaded wagons, slogging through the axle-deep mud, rushing east. Word was that Santa Anna had vowed to slaughter every Anglo west of the Sabine River.

And if that wasn't bad enough, we reached Goliad in time to see General Urrea and his soldiers marching a captured Fannin and his men back into the fort. We didn't have time to see much more, for a patrol of the Delores Cavalry spotted us and gave chase.

We hit a creek bottom, and I sent Robert north to Houston. I waited until the patrol spotted me, then headed south, leading the Santanistas away from Robert. After a few miles, I was pulling away from them when Horse stumbled crossing a small gully, flipping me head over heels into the tall grass. He came up limping.

I hated to lose the mustang, but my choices were severely limited. I slapped him on the rump and dived into the grass. Moments later, the patrol swept past, still pursuing Horse.

Grinning, I rose to my feet and looked around. My grin froze. Coming straight toward me was the entire blasted Santanista army. I ducked under the nearest windfall and waited for dark.

Chapter Four

The gunshot jerked me awake. I bolted upright, searching for my handgun. Then I spotted Susanna Zuber standing stock still, her face frozen in shock and my pistol in her hand, staring at a small fire in the grass behind me.

"What the—" I leaped to my feet, yanked the pistol from her hand, at the same time shoving her away from the burning grass. And then I started stomping and yelling. Smoke filled the tent, stinging our eyes, choking our throats. Finally, the fire was extinguished. I spun on the girl, but she had her head buried in Kate's neck, sobbing as if her heart was broken.

Personally, I was ready to break something else. "What the Sam Hill do you think you were doing, girl?" I leaned forward, jutting out my jaw.

The other girls gathered fearfully behind Kate, who glared at me. "Stop shouting at the girl. Can't you see she's sorry?" Gently, she patted Susanna's back, consoling her with soft murmurings. "Besides, no one was hurt."

I hesitated. The rain beat heavily on the tarp above us. A rumble of thunder rolled past. "What if the Santanistas heard the shot? You think of that?" I glared back at Kate.

She rolled her eyes. "With all this thunder and rain? I doubt it."

Her calm and unruffled demeanor enraged and infuriated me, so I did what any man would do. I waved the pistol over my head and shouted. "These things are dangerous. She could have killed someone." I figured those two statements might elicit some serious concern from Kate.

She replied quietly, "I know, but she didn't. And she promises never to touch them again." She added stiffly, "And stop shouting. You're making more noise than the pistol."

Clenching my teeth, I suppressed the string of curses dying to leap out. My eyes narrowing, I stared hard at Susanna. "Don't you ever touch one of my guns again, you hear?"

She dropped her chin to her chest and nodded imperceptibly. "Yessir," she muttered. Tears rolled down her cheeks.

I looked back at Kate. Our eyes locked. Sparks flew,

and lightning flashed between us inside the tent. Lowering my voice, I said, "Now, we best get us some sleep."

I awakened a few hours later to absolute blackness. The rain had stopped; the fire had died out. A chill had settled in. I lay motionless, listening to the steady breathing behind me.

Suddenly, Uncle Ned's gentle voice eased through the darkness in a whisper. "You reckon we should be moving out, Mr. Walker, sir?"

Surprised he knew I was awake, I didn't reply for a few seconds.

He continued, "Can't never tell where Santa Anna's soldiers gonna be. I sure don't want these here girls to get caught up by them Mexican soldiers."

I replied in a like whisper, "Me neither, Ned. Me neither." After a moment's pause, I answered his question. "I reckon you're right. We need to get you started for the Sabine."

"Yessir." He hesitated. "You ain't going with us, Mr. Walker?"

I sensed a note of disappointment in his tone, and for some reason I felt guilty. My cheeks burned, and I was grateful for the darkness. "No, Ned. I got to reach General Houston. He's building an army to fight Santa Anna. It's my duty as a Texican to defend Texas."

A moment of silence, then, "Yessir."

I heard him stirring. A tiny red dot appeared in the darkness, and moments later, a small flame leaped up, pushing aside the night. Without a word, I rolled my soogan, shivering against the briskness of the early morning. When I finished, I looked at Ned. "I'll hook up the team. Why don't you wake the girls?"

I stomped through the mud to the team, grateful for the brogans on my feet. I usually carried moccasins in my saddlebag, but that kind of footwear wasn't much use in all this mud.

The oxen were gentle animals, unlike some of the mules and horses I had rigged in the past. Since I didn't have to worry about getting my head kicked in or a leg busted by some addle-brained broomtail, my thoughts strayed as I backed the docile beasts in place and hooked the trace chains to the singletrees.

I began having second thoughts about joining Houston, at least right away.

The idea of leaving an old man and five girls out in the middle of Texas didn't appeal to me, in spite of my sense of duty. The Santanistas were bad enough, but toss in marauding Comanches, maybe a few wandering Cherokees from East Texas, and the small party wouldn't have any more of a chance than a circuit preacher playing a cardsharp with a stacked deck.

Behind me came the sounds of the camp being dismantled amid the muffled whispers of the children. Once or twice, one of the girls sniffled. Jenny, I guessed, wondering just what had happened to her brother.

With Ned's help, I lashed the toolbox to the yoke and stowed the girls' gear. The short-haul wagon was an odd-looking sight in the early morning light, its stubby bed extending beyond the seat four feet.

Kate had bundled herself and the girls in blankets against the crisp air. I lifted Susanna onto the seat, and the other three I placed on the bed, rearranging the gear around them. "Now you, Miss Kate. You and Ned hop up on the seat."

From her perch, she looked down at me. "Well, good luck, Mr. Walker."

I glanced over my shoulder toward Gonzales, then looked back at her. There was still tension between us, but I knew what I had to do. "Well, if you don't mind, I think I'll ride along with you for a few miles. I can always head north. Maybe we'll find some more folks up ahead for you to join up with."

She studied me for several seconds just as if she were sizing up a piece of beef or a horse. "We'd be right pleased to have you along." She handed Ned a blanket. "Wrap yourself up good, Uncle Ned."

I hooked my thumb toward the rising sun. "Isn't Victoria back that way somewhere?"

Kate nodded. "About a day's ride or so."

"Let's try for there," I said. "Maybe we can find some other folks. You can't tell, maybe your own families are waiting there for you."

* * *

With me leading the way and Ned handling the reins, we wound through the underbrush until we reached the prairie, a basin twenty or so miles wide thick with bunchgrass and prickly pear. Off to the south a couple of miles, a line of trees meandered to the east, probably following a watercourse.

That was our destination. If the Santanistas caught us out in the middle of the prairie, we wouldn't have a chance. The smart route would be near timber so we could duck inside if we spotted any danger.

For some reason, I was surprised that Kate said nothing as I pointed us toward the trees. Despite her cool regard, her little flare-up the night before still disturbed me, but since we weren't going to be around each other much longer, I decided to shrug it off.

The days of rain had turned the prairie to a morass of calf-deep mud. The iron rims cut deep into the oozing mixture, but the oxen pulled steadily, and just as steadily we drew closer to the treeline and turned east.

I turned back to the cart. "Ned, stay close to the trees. If you see anyone, anyone at all, pull into the trees and wait." I nodded to the rifle leaning against the seat between Kate and Ned. "Check your powder and keep that handy."

With a brief nod, Ned asked, "Where you going, Mr. Walker?"

Motioning to the east, I replied, "To scout ahead. See what might be waiting for us." Glancing at the suffused glow of the sun through the gray clouds overhead, I guessed it was close to noon. "I'll be back before sundown. If I can find a trail, we'll ride on into the night as long as we can see."

Kate nodded. "Be careful."

Surprised at her concern, I hesitated, glanced at her, then nodded.

The countryside appeared deserted. I kept expecting tracks, a sign of passing wagons, but apparently we were off the main routes. Leaving the treeline after a couple of hours, I cut across the prairie, heading northeast. I was taking a gamble, but the chances of cutting a trail made it seem worthwhile.

Off to my left, the prairie seemed to rise. I ignored it. That was my first mistake. Buffalo wallows dot the western plains. Deep impressions in the prairie created by thousands, maybe even hundreds of thousands of buffaloes rolling in the sand, a wallow can sometimes reach the depth of six or seven feet. More than once, I'd camped in a wallow, the circular walls breaking the constant prairie wind.

Without warning, a rifle boomed behind me. I jerked around to see three Santanistas astride their horses standing on top of the wallow. One shouted. The other two had their *escopetas* aimed at me, which didn't worry me for the surplus English muzzleloaders could barely throw a slug seventy yards, and then with absolutely no accuracy. The only way one of those

Santanista jaspers could be sure of hitting the side of a barn was if they shot one of those muzzleloaders off *inside* the barn.

Instantly, I slammed my heels into my pony's flanks and leaned low over the saddle. The large warhorse seemed to take forever to reach a full gallop. The shouts behind told me the Santanistas had given chase.

I had no idea of the stamina of the horse I was riding, and I was concerned that those behind me might be driving me smack-dab into the middle of their entire army. Some distance to my right was a stand of oak timber that stretched for over a mile.

Glancing over my shoulder, I saw we were gaining on them. The prairie blurred beneath the large horse's feet and a film of mud thrown up by the galloping hooves began building on my legs. Leaning forward, I patted his neck. "That's it, boy. Stretch them legs." Slowly, I turned him in the direction of the timber, at the same time trying to formulate some kind of plan.

I could take shelter in the timber and ambush them, but the noise would carry. No telling what was beyond the timber. Or I could try to just outrun them, but then I couldn't afford to wear my pony out. No, my smartest move was to try to lose them.

Two hundred yards from the young timber, I cut directly toward the middle, grinning at the understory vegetation, thick with yaupon, wild huckleberries, grapevines, and gourds.

Tugging gently, I slowed, wanting the Santanistas

to draw closer. If I could wangle all three into following me into the tangle of underbrush, then maybe I could slow them enough for me to give them the slip.

I glanced over my shoulder. They were within thirty yards. Their warhorses carried bright armor and were by necessity large boned. I squeezed my knees against the horse's ribs. He shot forward.

Ahead, what appeared to be a small path led into the timber between two oaks. We flew down the trail, angling sharply back to the left within ten feet of the entrance. A deer trail, the path wound lazily through the timber and undergrowth. To my surprise, my remount stayed right on the trail.

Lying low on his neck, I gave him his head, letting him pick his way through the snarl of vines and shrubs. Maybe he could do a better job of it than me.

A startled scream from behind caught my attention. I glanced over my shoulder. Two Santanistas sat astride the first two chargers. The third saddle was empty, but the warhorse remained with the pack, carrying out his duty.

With a chuckle, I looked back around just in time to duck a low-hanging grapevine. Suddenly, there came a grunt, a frightened squeal, and the sound of bodies crashing through the underbrush following by startled cries from the Santanistas and terrified whinnies from the warhorses.

My animal kept his pace, and minutes later, we emerged on the prairie beyond the timber. I saw no

Santanistas anywhere. I saw no one, so I headed back to the cart, remaining near the timber.

Two or three times, I cut the trail of other settlers who had passed before us. Many walked, some had wagons, some horses, some pushed a few cows ahead of them.

I peered west, anxiously hoping to spot the oxen and cart.

An hour later, I spotted a lazy column of smoke drifting into the clouded sky. "I hope not," I muttered, unable to believe Kate would be so foolish as to build a fire in the middle of the day so everyone for miles around could see the smoke.

Easing just inside the timberline, I kept my pony in a slow walk. The timber was not old, for there was still much underbrush about, enough to hide me and enough to hide whoever laid the fire.

Suddenly, my horse's ears perked forward, and then he did a little stutter-step. "Easy, boy," I whispered, pulling him to a halt and sliding to the ground. "Just take it easy."

After checking my rifle and the two pistols in my belt, I slipped forward. The supple tips of huckleberry vines brushed over my poncho, making a wispy, feathery sound as I ghosted through the undergrowth.

I paused behind every tree, peering into the timber around me. Suddenly, I spotted the cart. The oxen were still yoked, but the cart was empty.

Chapter Five

I remained motionless behind a thick snarl of berry briars wrapped around a rotting log. The oxen stood contentedly. From where I was situated, I saw that all of the gear had been removed from the wagon. Off to the left, smoke drifted through the treetops and into the overcast sky above.

A brisk wind blew from the north, humming through the treetops, bringing with it a few drops of rain. Stealthily, I eased forward, searching the surrounding undergrowth for sentries at every step.

The wind caught the wood smoke and swirled it through the timber. With the pungent whiff of burning wood came the drift of laughter. I puzzled over the source of the sound. Santanistas? Maybe another small patrol like the one I eluded earlier.

I crept forward, straining to peer through the dense undergrowth. Abruptly, I dropped to one knee behind a patch of wild huckleberries. My throat was dry; my heart thudded against my chest.

In a small clearing beyond the wild huckleberries stood three rough-looking men—two Anglos and one Mexican, a fat one. Scavengers, I guessed, depraved vermin who stole from those less fortunate, men so low they had to stand on a pickle barrel just to kiss a rattlesnake's belly. One Anglo wore a stovepipe hat, the other one of those little black derbies. The Mexican wore a sombrero.

Kate and the girls huddled together against the drizzle next to the trunk of a lightning-shattered oak. The girls had buried their faces in Kate's outspread arms. Naturally, Jenny Adkins was crying. Kate soothed her, at the same time glaring at the three scavengers defiantly.

Uncle Ned, his arms filled with logs for the fire, stumbled through the mud while the Mexican yelled at him. The Anglos laughed. One turned up a jug of whiskey and guzzled several mouthfuls, spilling it down his throat and onto his greasy leather shirt.

Suddenly, I began to tremble. I'd been scared before, but nothing like this. What the scavengers had planned for Kate and the girls was obvious. Uncle Ned? They'd probably kill him.

I'd never killed a man. Shot at a few marauding Comanche, but even then, I hadn't hit one. Or if I did, it was nothing more than a flesh wound, for not a single one ever fell from the back of his war pony.

My breath came faster. My heart pumped like a windmill. I glanced down. My rifle and pistols were out of the rain under my poncho, but still, the dampness could affect them. I only had three shots. What if one misfired? Moving silently, I hurried back to my pony where I reloaded all three weapons. Momentarily, I laid my hand on the hilt of my bowie. I hoped I didn't have to resort to it. I hurried back to the camp, kneeling behind a wild azalea.

During my absence, the Anglo in the stovepipe hat had moved around the fire and stood over Kate, leering down at her. "Well, little missy. Why don't you turn loose of them crybabies? Let's just see how friendly you can be."

She hissed and crouched lower, like a mountain lion ready to spring. "Don't touch me." Her eyes blazed.

He laughed and grabbed at her.

Uncle Ned had been crouched by the fire, feeding it logs. When the Anglo grabbed at Kate, Ned shouted and struggled to his feet. Before he could take a step, the grinning Mexican slammed his pistol against the old man's head. Ned crumpled.

The time for backing and filling was past. Now the time had come for action. I knew what I had to do, but I just hoped I could do it. In one smooth movement, I jammed the butt of my Long Tom into my shoulder and squeezed off a shot. My rifle roared, and a plume of blue smoke filled the air. My .45 ball knocked Stovepipe's leg from under him, spinning him around and hurling him to the mud.

The girls screamed.

Instantly, I dropped my rifle against the azalea and pulled out my two pistols. "Keep your hands where I can see them, boys," I said very quietly as I stepped into the clearing. "These two little sisters in my hands carry enough lead to tear a hole in your belly big enough to stick your fist in."

From the corner of my eye, I could make out Stovepipe rolling back and forth in the mud, screaming and moaning, his hands clutching his leg.

Kate rushed to Ned. The girls started after her. Keeping my eyes on the two scavengers, I shouted, "Stop right there, girls. Don't go any farther." I grinned wickedly at the two men. "I don't want anybody in the way when I kill these two jaspers."

Their eyes grew wide. The Anglo's face blanched behind his thick beard. "Hold on, Mister. Don't shoot. We ain't done nothing to you. Give us a break."

"Like you gave that old man a break?"

The fat Mexican gulped. Despite the cold, sweat ran down his face. "Please, *Señor. Por la gracia de Dios.*"

Ned stirred.

"All right, boys. Drop your pistols and knives."

They did as I asked.

"Now, you—with the derby hat. Get your friends's weapons. And don't try anything foolish." I eased to my left so I could watch him. Moments later, he tossed Stovepipe's pistol and knife in the mud with his.

I gestured to the Mexican. "Now, you. Over with your friends."

By now, Ned was sitting up. The side of his head was beginning to swell. "Okay, girls. Help Miss Kate get Ned back to the cart."

After they left, I slipped one of the pistols under my belt. I studied the three scavengers. Leaving them without weapons was certain death if the Santanistas caught up with them. And as much as they deserved whatever fate they met, I didn't want it on my conscience.

With a grin, I knelt and stuck two of the pistols under my belt. I pulled the percussion caps off the remaining weapons, and then proceeded to grind the pistols and rifles under the mud with my foot. By the time they cleaned them out and reloaded, we'd be long gone. Besides, I planned on taking their ponies. I gathered the reins.

The Anglo wearing the derby took a step forward. "You can't leave us without horses. It ain't right."

"Maybe *I* ain't right. You ever think about that? You just best be glad I'm leaving your guns. One more word from you, I'll take them." With that, I swung into the saddle of a nice bay. I looked down at the surly trio. "Come after us, and I'll kill you certain." I wheeled the bay around and headed back through the timber for my pony, leading the two remaining horses behind me.

Minutes later, I caught up with the cart, which Kate had started moving eastward along the edge of the muddy prairie. The girls stared at me wide-eyed. And for once, Jenny Adkins wasn't crying. Leaning over, I tied the horses' reins to the rear of the cart and remained on the bay. "How's Ned feeling?"

The old man grinned up at me. "I'm fine, Mr. Walker."

The tips of my ears burned. I grinned sheepishly. "The name's Bob. 'Mister' makes me feel like my old man, Ned."

He chuckled, and Kate smiled faintly. She glanced over our back trail. "What about them?"

To the west, the sun set behind the gray clouds. "Well, we got their ponies, and by the time they clean the mud out of their pistols and rifles, we'll be long gone." I studied the prairie off to our left. "I reckon we ought to keep moving for another couple of hours before making a cold camp. I don't suspect those three will follow, but no sense in taking any chances."

The clouds remained thick. With the setting of the sun sometime later, night descended quickly. I studied the heavy cloud cover, then pointed to the timber off to our right. "Pull in over there. I got a feeling we're going to be blind as newborn kittens in a few minutes."

Within a short time, we pulled up in a small clearing

and stretched tarps against the chill of the oncoming night. I staked out the ponies and oxen while the girls spread a tarp and quilts on top, after which they unpacked our meager supply of grub.

By the time they climbed under the tarps, absolute blackness had crept over the countryside. So dark, we couldn't see the body next to us. So dark, we had to feel for the outstretched hand holding out the cornbread or cold pork.

I wrapped my blanket around me and leaned up against a small oak. I relaxed. If we couldn't see our hands before our eyes, no one else could either.

Still, I slept in bits and pieces. Early in the morning, I awakened and spotted shafts of starlight streaming through the treetops and splashing across the forest floor. I rose quickly, making my way to the edge of the timber. The sky had cleared.

Five minutes later, we were moving. The starlight illumined the prairie with a bluish glow. I pulled up beside the wagon. "We can stop after the sunrise and build a small fire. Maybe whip up a hot broth or something."

One of the girls whispered, "I'd like that."

Another replied, "I'm so cold. Hot broth sounds wonderful."

I glanced over my shoulder. Far behind, I thought I saw small moving shadows. I reined the bay up and peered into the night behind us. Nothing. Just my imagination, I told myself.

For once, luck went our way. Just before sunrise, we rode up on a small log cabin tucked away in a copse of oak and pecan. Behind the cabin was a barn, a smokehouse, and well house. A few fat hogs grunted and jumped to their feet, staring at us before dashing toward the barn. A dozen or so chickens roosted in the trees. In one corner of the yard, I spotted a nest of eggs. A handful of cats ran toward us, mewing, and a gaunt hound lay back warily, barking dolefully.

Kate and me exchanged looks. I shrugged, dismounted, and climbed up on the porch. A sign was fastened to the door with a wooden peg.

> Gon to U-Nited Staz. Bak wen
> Mexcans an Santanner is gon. Tak
> whut you ned. Klos Door wen you leav.
>
> J. B. Burlmayer

I grinned back at Kate and Ned. "We're in luck. Good neighbor Burlmayer here has invited us to share his grub . . . if there's any left," I added.

There was half a sack of coffee beans and a bag of shucked corn in the larder. Out in the smokehouse hung several slabs of bacon. We took one, leaving the others. Thick, green mold covered the pork, keeping the meat beneath fresh. Susanna gathered the eggs. Mary, Kate's little sister, found two more nests with a dozen eggs plus a four-foot length of rawhide lariat which she decided would serve as a small whip.

Kate stared wistfully at the mud-and-stick fireplace. "I've forgotten what it was like to spend the night under a roof."

Towheaded Dilue Harris chirped up. "Oh, yes, yes. Let's spend the night."

The girls chimed in. "Let's spend the night. Oh, please, please," they begged in unison.

Dilue held up her rag doll to me. "Please, Mr. Walker. Cassie wants to sleep in a real bed tonight."

I shook my head. "Can't afford the chance, child. The smart thing for us is to move a few miles on, then find a hidey-hole where we can put together a smokeless fire. At least we can have a hot breakfast."

Uncle Ned agreed. "Mr. Bo . . . I mean, Bob is right, Miss Kate. This here place is a waitin' trap. We need to leave as fast as we can."

And we did, but first I laid four bits on the rough mantel over the fireplace.

Kate frowned at me. "Won't the next folks who come in here take it?"

"Not if they're common folk like us." I shook my head. "But if it's the Santanistas or the scavengers, yeah. They'll pocket it with a grin. At least we'll know we made the effort to be honest."

In addition to the grub, we found a couple of sunbonnets for the girls. For a brief moment, they squabbled over who could wear them, but Kate quickly settled the argument by giving one to teary-eyed Jenny Adkins and the other to Dilue Harris. "They're the two youngest," she announced flatly.

As we were loading our gear, I suggested Kate ride one of the horses. "Two of us casting around can see a lot more than just one set of eyes. Ned can drive the cart. We'll take the other two horses with us. No telling when an extra pony or two will come in handy."

So, with Kate on a black and me on the bay and Ned driving the cart, we struck out, angling to the southeast and Victoria, always remaining close to the timber just in case we had to hide in a hurry.

Two hours later, we camped, and laid a small fire under a thick canopy of oak limbs so the smoke would be scattered into the clear sky. We boiled coffee, broiled bacon, fried eggs, and fried spoon bread. Meager fare, but to us it was like feasting in one of those English kings' castles.

Ned and I stood while we all ate, the two of us keeping our eyes moving across the plains.

"How far do you suppose we are from Victoria? About half a a day?" Kate asked between mouthfuls of egg and bacon.

I shrugged. "Maybe we'll be there by tonight, but no sense taking any chances. We'll hide out in a safe place, and I'll slip in and see what's taking place."

If I'd known then what I learned later, I could have saved us five or six days of riding and a run-in with four Comanches and a crazy mountain man who must've tossed down one too many glasses of whiskey.

Chapter Six

Leaving the small group snug in a copse of pecan and elm, I rode through the timber for over a mile before I cut across the prairie toward Victoria. My trail was obvious, but if someone back-trailed me, they'd lose the sign among the elm and pecan.

Fifteen minutes out on the prairie, the bay's ears perked. He tossed his head and whinnied without missing a gait. I looked around us, searching the horizon.

Suddenly, a cold chill rolled over me. Far to my right came the Mexican army, on an angle to intercept me had I continued. I jerked my animal to a halt, quickly studying my predicament. They were still so distant, they appeared as only dark knots on the prairie. The columns stretched back over the southwestern horizon. Only Santa Anna had an army of such size.

Quickly, I dismounted and pulled my pony to the ground. I lay behind him, laying my hand over his muzzle so he wouldn't whinny and hoped the Santanista sentries had not spotted us. I glanced at the clear sky. Where in the blazes was rain when you wanted it? We'd had days of torrential downpours, and now . . . I held my breath and watched.

To my relief, no one rode toward us, but the column was so long, it took almost an hour to disappear over the eastern horizon.

Were they heading to Victoria? General Houston had wanted Fannin to defend Victoria. Maybe when he learned of Fannin's fate, he'd sent another company to the small village. For a moment, my hopes surged. Maybe there was still time for me to get into the fight. But on second thought, I knew better. I had Kate and the girls, and Ned. I couldn't abandon them.

Mounting the bay, I drove him into a gallop. At least now we knew where the Santanistas were, which meant we went in the other direction.

Wasting no time, we cut southeast, planning on crossing the Guadalupe River far below Victoria, and then cutting across the prairie to Brazoria on the Brazos River.

We reached the river just before dark. I had no idea how far we were below Victoria, but I could hear no rifle nor cannon fire, and the Santanista cannons could be heard for a distance of fifty or sixty miles.

The Guadalupe has its headwaters in the Texas Hill Country. The water is icy and blue, but at flood stage, it turns brown and ugly, carrying huge drift logs that sweep away everything in their path. And we had no ferries, not in our neck of the woods.

I stood on the bank staring across the hundred-foot-wide river. Kate stopped at my side. "How do we get across?"

Slowly, I shook my head.

"Too bad we don't have enough rope. We could swim the oxen to the far bank and then they could pull the wagon across."

"Yeah," I muttered, puzzling over our predicament.

"We can build us a raft," said Ned, coming up behind us.

I looked around at the elderly man, his shoulders stooped, his curly white hair lying close against his skull. His dark eyes blazed with confidence. "Yessir. We can built us a dandy-fine raft." He pointed downriver. "Look yonder. See how the river, she curves like a horseshoe?"

A few hundred yards downriver, the Guadalupe swept to the right and curved back toward us. "Yeah. So what?" I had no idea what the old man had in mind.

"Easy as sweet potato pie. We take your rope and them on the scavengers' horses to tie logs to all four sides of the wagon, then drift down to the curl. We drift right into the bank. See, like them drift logs done."

Several logs had jammed into the far bank. As we watched, the current pulled a log from the mud and swept it around the curve in the river. Kate and me exchanged surprised looks. No reason it wouldn't work. I grinned at Ned. "We got a saw. The oxen can haul the logs down to the shore. Then I can swim the oxen over and come back.

"We'll start at first light," I said.

The night was cold. And we were miserable, but we all looked forward to the next day. At sunrise, we all pitched in. Susanna, being the oldest of the children, looked after the girls while Kate, Ned, and me cut and rolled the heavy logs into the water, quickly fastening them in the shape of a box around the short-haul wagon. We tied it to an ancient willow against the heavy current.

Wrapping my rifle, pistols in my poncho, I gave them to Kate. "Keep your rifle out and the powder dry just in case."

She nodded, and we both scanned the empty countryside around us. I climbed on the bay, gathered the reins of the other ponies, and urged the oxen into the river. Immediately, the current pushed us downriver, but the animals swam strongly. Within a hundred yards, we clambered ashore.

Quickly, I led the animals up the bank and tied them to some scrub oak. I entered the river far above the raft.

The current was fierce. At first I thought I would be swept past the raft, but at the last second, I grabbed one of the ropes on the raft and pulled myself aboard. I lay motionless, catching my breath.

Ned had cut him and me some long push poles. Kate and the girls climbed up on the wagon. I looked at Ned. "Ready?"

He gave me a warm grin, and his eyes danced with excitement. "Yessir. I'm ready."

I cut the rope and the current caught us. The girls screamed, but Kate silenced them immediately. I glanced at her, and our eyes met. She gave me a funny smile, one I couldn't figure out just what it meant. But I quickly forgot about it as water sloshed and splashed around my ankles. We strained against the poles. Slowly the raft edged closer to the far shore.

When we were three-quarters of the way across, Ned called out, "Mr. Bob, Mr. Bob. Look!"

He pointed upriver. The weather had uprooted a giant pecan tree, and it was bearing down on us. If it hit us, the tree would sweep right over us, shoving our raft underwater.

"Push, Ned. Push."

The roots of the tree stuck into the air like giant fingers splayed wide. The girls began to whimper. Kate's eyes were wide with fright. The tree was moving too fast. There was no way it would miss us.

I jammed my pole into the muddy bottom and

grunted mightily, straining to push the raft out of the path of certain catastrophe. Sweat rolled down my face. And the tree drew closer and closer.

His lips curled in a snarl, Ned squeezed his eyes shut as he exerted every ounce of strength he possessed against the pole. He tried to grip the pole with his twisted hand, and the tendons in the back of his good hand stood out like banjo strings from clenching the pole so tightly.

I yelled at Kate, "When it hits, grab the girls. Maybe we can stay afloat."

Without warning, a rope snaked through the air from the far shore and settled over the thickest of the roots. A moment later, the rope stretched taut, water popping off it as it hummed with tension. I glanced to the far shore where the rope disappeared into a tangle of berry vines and small willows.

Ned and I exchanged looks, then jumped back to our task. The rope couldn't hold too long. By now, we were almost out of the path of the tree. Suddenly, with the sound like the report of a pistol, the rope snapped. For a moment, the pecan lay motionless, and then continued downriver.

"Push, Ned. Push," I groaned between clenched teeth.

Kate and the girls watched mesmerized as the tree came closer and closer.

At the last minute, we slipped from its path as the

raging current swept it past. Moments later, we rammed into the muddy shore.

"Howdy, folks. That were a close one, huh?"

I looked around to see a bearded old man in buckskins and wearing a coonskin cap grinning at us from shore. He swayed his head slowly from one side to the other and wore a steady grin on his face. He leaned his long rifle against a willow and waded into the water with another rope, which he tied to the wagon tongue. "Yessir," he continued, "that was about as close as I ever see'd." Still nodding from side to side, he held out his hand for Kate. "Best come on off, ma'am, afore the water takes it again." His cheerful grin revealed a set of maybe half-a-dozen or so teeth.

"Much obliged, Mister," I said, wading to shore, half spooked by the strange hombre. I pointed into the timber. "Appreciate the help. I got us some oxen in here that'll get the wagon out."

"Yep. See'd them too." He began helping the girls off while I retrieved the oxen.

Within minutes, we had the wagon ashore and back into the timber.

I extended my hand. "Much obliged again, Mister. My name's Bob Walker." I introduced him to the others.

He gave us a gap-toothed smile and held up his left hand. "The Indians call me Joe Two-Fingers." His middle two fingers were nubs. "Lost them in a dynamite blast."

The girls stared at him in awe. I couldn't help noticing the bones dangling from the cord around his neck, bones that looked a lot like finger bones. But I didn't say anything.

He continued, pointing at his left shoulder. "An' this cantankerous old bird is Windingo. I call him Winnie for short. He don't like the name, but he's stuck with it."

I blinked, then gaped at his shoulder. There was nothing there. We all looked at each other in confusion. The girls edged away from Joe Two-Fingers, taking refuge behind Kate who was eyeing the old mountain man with a healthy dose of wariness. I cleared my throat. "Winnie? Where?"

He laughed. "Why, son, right here on my shoulder. Oh, yeah, folks say I'm tetched." He tapped a gnarled finger against his forehead. "But I ain't, leastwise no more'n the next hombre. Besides, how come you figure I managed to live all them years with Indians?"

"Well, Joe Two-Fingers, I wish we had time to share pleasantries, but we got the whole Santanista army on our trail. We're heading for Brazoria. You're welcome to ride along with us if you got a mind to."

Kate shot me a startled look.

Joe studied Kate and the girls. Still several feet from the girls, he knelt so he could talk to them at their level. Still swaying his head from side to side, he spoke to Windingo. "Whatta you think, Winnie?

Should we go? Maybe not. I think them little girls is scared of us."

The startled expression on Kate's face faded into a gentle smile. She squeezed her little sister's shoulder in reassurance. Mary glanced up at Kate. Seeing the smile on her sister's lips, the little red-haired girl grinned. "No, sir, Mr. Joe Two-Fingers. We ain't scared of you." She glanced at her friends for confirmation.

For a moment, no one moved, then as one, they all shook their heads emphatically. "Oh, no," exclaimed Susanna. "We ain't scared." But she eyed his bone necklace warily.

Joe Two-Fingers was afoot, so we offered him one of the scavengers' ponies, a sorrel. Now with three of us on horseback, casting far and wide from the rattling old cart, we rode toward Brazoria with our minds a little more at rest.

Mid-morning, I noticed the ground at our feet was growing spongy. From time to time, a tangy drift of salt air stung my nostrils. I pulled up beside Kate. "You familiar with this part of the country?"

She looked up at me. "No."

"Well, I think we need to cut north. From the lay of the land and the smell in the air, I figure we're heading into the saltwater marshes. Back north, we'll hit solid ground again."

I rode over to the cart and told Ned.

He grunted. "Yessir. I see'd salt marsh before. They swallow a body up to feed the 'gators."

By dusk, we'd moved five or six miles inland, beyond the saltwater marshes. Just how far, I wasn't sure, but the footing was firm. We set up camp a hundred yards or so north of a freshwater pool. I wouldn't have minded camping closer to the water, but then we might have had a sleeping partner in the form of a curious alligator. And that was a chance I didn't want to take. I'd heard more than my share of stories of big 'gators snatching sleeping dogs or humans out of a camp and dragging them back into the water.

Joe Two-Fingers rode in minutes after we laid the fire. "Ain't nothing north of us but deer and bear." His head swaying, he scooted around in his saddle and laid his hand on the plump haunches of a whitetail deer. "And I got us a nice fat one."

I rose quickly. Before I could say a word, he added, "Don't fret, Bob. I didn't shoot it."

Before I could question him, he flipped the deer to the ground and dismounted. "I'll dress him out after I put up this pony." He patted the sorrel on the rump. "Game little animal here, Bob. Sure-footed. Deep chest."

Kate glanced at me and dipped her head toward the old mountain man. Taking her hint, I said, "He's yours, Joe. We took him off some scavengers. Someone might as well get some use from him."

He looked around at us in surprise. "Well, now,

that's mighty nice of you folks. And I do appreciate it."

Fashioning a tarp around the inland side of the camp to shield the fire, we roasted deer, mixed up corn mush, and boiled coffee.

The sky remained clear, and the stars popped out so thick a body would never be able to count them all. As we sprawled lazily around the cheery fire, I asked Joe about the deer. "How'd you kill it if you didn't shoot it?"

He grinned slyly and tapped his finger to his forehead that continued to move from side to side. "Indian trick. Deer are mighty curious," he said, grinning at the girls. "So, I tie my knife to a strong stick and a piece of red cloth to another stick. Then I cover myself up with my buffalo robe. Them deer get so curious, they come up to sniff at the piece of waving cloth. They get that close, I drive my knife into them." He grinned. "All nice and quiet."

Ned frowned at me. I nodded. "I hear tell of the Apache killing antelope like that. I reckon deer are as curious."

"Yessir," replied Joe. "Curious as can be." He hesitated. "You folks seem to be a long ways from nowhere."

"Yep. There's big trouble in Texas right now. We're trying to stay out of it, if we can." I brought Joe up to date on our situation, about the Santanistas, General

Houston, and the panic that was driving Texans to the Sabine River.

The girls clustered around Kate, their eyes stealing curious looks at Joe Two-Fingers, who, head swaying, from time to time muttered cryptic phrases to Winnie.

"What about when you folks get to Brazoria? What then? How do you know them Santanistas ain't there?"

The shocked expression on Kate's face told me she hadn't considered that option. I had, but I figured we'd play that just like we had Victoria. Camp out in the boondocks, sneak in, find out what was going on, then act from there.

I gave her a reassuring grin. "Depends on what we find at Brazoria."

Joe muttered something to Winnie. The rest of us lapsed into a curious silence. We were anxious to learn more about our new companion, but good manners forbade us asking. If he wanted us to know, he'd volunteer the information.

Sometimes the brash naiveté of children has its advantages. Mary Rusk burst out, "Are you a real mountain main, Mr. Two-Fingers?"

Joe stared at the girl from under his bushy eyebrows. He stroked his thick, black beard. Instinctively, the girls pressed up against Kate. I spotted a glimmer of amusement in Joe's eyes. Without taking his eyes off Mary, he spoke to Winnie. "Reckon we ought to tell her, huh, Winnie?"

He cocked his ear as if listening, then nodded. "I

suppose it won't hurt nothing. Sure you don't mind?"

Joe listened a few moments, then grunted. "Might as well." He placed his elbows on the saddle behind him and leaned back, working his lanky body back and forth to get comfortable. His head kept moving. "Yep, little lady. I reckon you can say I'm a mountain man. One that got his fill and was ready to come home, except to find that what was once home ain't there no more."

He went on to tell us of how he joined the Salmon and Fur Trade Company, comprised of fifty-eight men, counting four priests, a botanist, and an ornithologist. He told us of his life in the Rocky Mountains, up in the Bighorns, the Tetons, the Absaroka Range; of the Hunkpapa, the Snake, the Crow, the Washaki, and dozens of other tribes. He fascinated us with stories of fat beaver, ferocious grizzlies, majestic elk. He regaled us with the feats of mountain men and explorers like Jedediah Smith, Bill Sublette, John Colter, and François Larocque.

Finally, he fell silent.

The fire had burned low. The wood popped and crackled, sending tiny red coals arching through the air. "Then after the last rendezvous at Fort Walla Walla on the Columbia River, I decided it was time for me to come home."

Susanna Zuber leaned forward, her freshly scrubbed face gleaming in the firelight. "I reckon they was sure glad to see you, huh, Mr. Two-Fingers. Huh?"

His expression didn't change, but for the first time since we met him, he held his head still. "No, child. They wasn't there. Not alive that is. I found their graves. Pa and Ma. My brother Aaron, and his wife, who I never knowed. They was drowned in a big flood in '28. At least that's what them words cut into the headboard said. The house was gone. Someone had built another one farther from the river. I reckon it belonged to whoever took over Ma and Pa's place."

He lapsed into silence.

The fire burned low.

A small voice cut through the stillness of the night. It was Dilue Harris. "Kate, Cassie wants a drink of water."

Kate murmured sleepily. "In the morning, Dilue. Have Cassie wait until morning."

For a moment, I forgot who Cassie was. Then I remembered. She was the little towheaded girl's rag doll. "Yeah. And none of you girls go outside tonight. You hear?"

With that, I pulled my blanket up over my shoulders.

Soon we all dropped off to sleep.

When we awakened the next morning, Dilue Harris and her rag doll were missing.

Chapter Seven

I jerked upright when I heard Kate shout. I looked around to see her holding an empty blanket. Then I realized she was screaming that Dilue Harris was missing. The first thought that leaped into my mind was alligators. Had one lumbered into camp while we slept?

Leaping to my feet, I raced to the water, not really knowing what I would find or what I should look for.

Joe Two-Fingers was right behind me, muttering under his breath to Winnie.

"Look," I exclaimed, pointing out two tiny heel marks in the mud on the bank of the pool. "She squatted here."

Kate caught her breath. She pressed her hands to her lips. "Oh, no, no."

I peered out across the pool, across the motionless reeds, but nothing broke the silvery expanse of water. Frustration welled up in me.

"Here. Over here," Joe half-shouted, half-whispered.

My blood ran cold. Beside Dilue's footprints were moccasin tracks, wide, flat-footed. Indian prints.

Joe squatted, studied the sign, his head swaying. "Only one of them, Winnie," he mumbled. "Must've been scoutin' us." He looked up at me. "Look around. See if there's more sign."

Kate laid her hand on my arm. "Oh, Bob. What are we going to do?"

I fixed her with what I hoped was a look of self-confidence. "We're going to find her and get her back. That's exactly what we're going to do."

"Here's another set," shouted Ned, several feet away.

"And here's where they met a third," added Joe. We followed the trail into a copse of scrub oak where they left their ponies. The sign was clear. The three of them, with Dilue, were heading back toward the Guadalupe.

"What do you figure, Joe? Comanche?"

"Can't tell. Were they Snake or Hunkpapa, I could spot them from the way they walk, but I ain't no common familiar with them Indians down here."

We peered across the tall grass prairie to the west, and as we did, dark clouds rolled over the northern horizon. I muttered a curse. Joe Two-Fingers grinned crookedly at me. He rocked his head from side to side. "Nothing to fret. Just one of them icy northers. Freeze ever'thing up good. Ain't that right, Winnie?"

We moved our camp into the scrub oak where Ned, Kate, and the girls would set up the tarps and gather wood against the coming storm. With Joe standing behind me, his head swaying slowly, the same grin on his face, I gave Ned and Kate instructions. "You've got rifles, powder, and lead. If we're not back when the storm clears, move on out. Head east. We'll find you."

Kate pushed the shawl from her head. Her red hair tumbled out. "Please find Dilue," she whispered.

I grinned. "Don't worry. We'll bring her back."

She laid her hand on my arm. "And be careful."

The grin faded from my lips, and I was suddenly aware of a strange feeling in my chest. I nodded briefly. "Don't worry."

The trail was easy to follow across the tallgrass prairie. We loped our ponies, an easy, bounding gait that ate up the miles. We'd both checked rifles and pistols before we left. Joe carried six ball-and-cap pistols plus his long rifle. Between the two of us, we had ten shots before reloading.

Late afternoon, the wind shifted. A brisk breeze danced across the heads of the prairie grass, and from the crest of a rolling hill, the gusts of wind appeared like giant footsteps striding across the prairie. The temperature began to drop.

I urged my pony to a faster pace. The little tow-headed girl had only the clothes on her back. Her blanket was back in camp, and the last thing one of those that stole her would do was worry about her well-being.

We rode faster. The wind stung my face, numbing my cheeks, but we rode without flinching. Slowly, the treeline of the Guadalupe peeked above the horizon. Without hesitation, we continued toward the trees. A few minutes later, Joe pulled up. Far to the west and north, a faint drift of smoke threaded upward from the treeline, unseen in clear sky, but visible against the backdrop of dark clouds rolling in.

He sat astride his sorrel, head wagging, muttering to Winnie. I spoke up. "What do you think?"

Without hesitation, he replied, "Winnie says it ain't them."

I eyed Joe skeptically. My first thought was just how that Windingo knew what it couldn't see. I hesitated, chiding myself. That crazy old mountain man almost had me believing that some kind of mystical creature perched on his shoulder. There was nothing on his shoulder. Nothing.

"Are you sure?"

Joe shrugged. "I ain't, but Winnie is mighty certain."

I eyed his shoulder again. Now, I didn't want to argue with that imaginary Windingo, but at the same time, I didn't want to go barging into an Indian camp and have them harm the child.

Before I could speak, Joe urged his sorrel into a gallop across the tallgrass prairie, directly toward the fire. I raced after him. "Joe!" I shouted when I pulled up beside the old man. "You're gonna get the child killed."

He cocked his head around and grinned. "I told you, son. That ain't their camp."

He was right.

As we approached the small camp, which was set back in a wash, Joe called out, "Hello, the camp! We be friends."

Two homespun-clad hombres, wearing Saltillo blankets, and an Indian in buckskins stepped from behind the broad boles of live oak and eyed us carefully before lowering the muzzles of their long rifles. I recognized one of the jaspers.

"Pleasant—Pleasant McAnella. That you?"

Surprised, he squinted up at me. "Well, Bob Walker! We'd done give you up for dead when you didn't get back from Goliad with Robert."

A sense of relief flooded over me. Robert had made it back to Sam Houston with word of Fannin's capture. I slid off my bay and gripped Pleasant's outstretched hand with a grin as broad as the Colorado River. I introduced Joe Two-Fingers, and met Pleasant's riding partner, Emmett Haywood. "And this," Pleasant added, "is Rides-With-Rain, a chief of the East Texas Cherokee nation. He come down with Houston, and General Sam sent him with us to make sure all the Texans are gone."

Rides-With-Rain grunted, his eyes fixed on Joe Two-Fingers, whose head continued swaying from side to side.

Pleasant indicated the coffee. "Sit a spell. Git some coffee." He shivered. "Reckon we're in for a cold night. You old boys might as well spend it here as out there," he said.

I grabbed a tin cup and tossed Joe one. "Thanks, but we got business." I poured Joe's coffee, then filled my cup. "We're after three Indians. They stole a little girl."

Pleasant and Emmett exchanged looks. Pleasant nodded to the Cherokee. "Rides-With-Rain spotted some a couple of hours back. Heading north. Comanche."

My hopes surged. I gulped the coffee and burned my mouth. Grimacing, I turned to Rides-With-Rain. "Can you show us the sign?"

He looked at Pleasant, then grabbed a heavy buffalo robe and slung it over his shoulders. "I go after child." He made a cutting motion with this hand to the north and spoke to Emmett and Pleasant. "You go back to Houston now. No more Texans here. All go to Sabine."

I glanced at Joe Two-Fingers who continued sipping on his coffee and mumbling under his breath to Winnie. Tossing my empty cup on the ground by the fire, I swung into the saddle. I grinned at Pleasant. "Soon as I take care of this job, I'll join you old boys. We'll pin Santa Anna to the ground until he hollers calf-rope."

Rides-With-Rain swung onto the back of a pinto and led out, swimming the Guadalupe and heading north along the river. Joe and me followed, riding well into the night until the sleet and rain hit.

I pulled up next to Rides-With-Rain. "We need to find a spot to hole up."

He pointed north. "No. We ride. We find the child soon."

I tugged my poncho tighter around me and ducked my head into the wind. How that Cherokee managed to stay on the trail, I'll never know. There were times on that blustery frigid night that I couldn't even see the ground at my horse's feet.

We rode for what seemed like hours as the sleet bounced off us, chilling our flesh to the bone. From time to time, spasms of shivering wracked my body. Abruptly, Rides-With-Rain pulled up and grunted. He pointed into the night at a flickering fire.

"She there?" I muttered.

He nodded. "Six, maybe seven Comanche."

I winced. I didn't want a shoot-out.

Rides-With-Rain turned to Joe. He pointed to the camp. "Crazy man get girl. Comanche no hurt."

Joe Two-Fingers grinned, understanding the Cherokee chief's suggestion. He nodded and whispered to me, "You and me swing around and come in from the north. Chief here stays put. That way, we got them on three sides with the river on the other."

Rides-With-Rain nodded tersely, and Joe and me started our swing around the camp.

A few minutes later, he dropped me off west of the camp. I could make out figures moving before the fire. That's when Joe Two-Fingers started babbling to Winnie, a stream of incoherent, inarticulate words. He kept it up until his words faded into the night.

Dismounting, I tied the bay to a low limb securely. In a crouch, I eased forward, searching the forest around me, trying to put the deadly cold from my mind. I doubted they had any sentries out, but if they did, I wanted to see him before he spotted me.

There were sudden exclamations at the camp. Rising to my feet, I pressed up against an elm and peered through the timber. I had a clear view. They were Comanche, six of them, and huddled beside the fire was Dilue Harris. She appeared well. I breathed a sigh of relief.

Without warning, Joe Two-Fingers rode into the Comanche camp on his sorrel, backward. I blinked in disbelief. He even wore his coonskin cap backward, the tail hanging in front of his bearded face. And he was babbling.

I jerked my long rifle to my shoulder, ready to shoot the first Comanche who attempted to kill Joe.

He reined up before the fire and calmly dismounted, backward, slinging his leg over his pony's head.

The Comanche were awestruck. They slowly lowered their weapons.

The old mountain man turned to the warriors. He held up his hand and spoke, but I couldn't make out the words. He gestured to his shoulder, and the startled Indians stared at one another.

I eased forward. I couldn't understand the words, but the sign was obvious. They asked Joe to sit and eat with them. Crossing his legs, he lowered himself to the ground as they squatted warily across the fire. One of the Comanche offered him a spit of broiling meat, but Joe declined, instead scooping up a handful of dirt and picking fingerfuls from it and dropping it in his mouth.

The warriors exchanged startled glances, then scooted back from the fire, obviously frightened of this crazy man who rode backward and ate dirt.

I stared, mesmerized by his performance. I'd heard that the Indian were superstitious of crazy men, but this was the first time I'd seen proof.

When Joe finished eating dirt, instead of washing in the river, he dipped up handfuls of sand and washed his hands, and then his face. Finally, patting his stomach, he rose.

Nervously, the Comanche rose, keeping their distance. They spoke to him, but he shook his head. And then, as if he'd just spotted the little girl, he grunted and pointed to her.

All the Comanche except one nodded instantly. He hesitated, shook his head.

Joe Two-Fingers turned to Winnie and spoke. He listened, nodded, and without warning, grabbed his knife and yanked it over his head and bellowed like an enraged grizzly at the single Indian warrior.

The Comanche stumbled backward, falling to the ground. Joe didn't move. Finally with the carriage of a king, he sheathed his knife, placed Dilue behind his saddle, facing the rear of the sorrel, climbed up behind her, and rode out of the camp.

I kept my rifle ready, just in case the downed Comanche changed his mind. He didn't. I waited ten minutes, then rode after Joe and the little girl.

We met where Rides-With-Rain was waiting. Quickly, we bundled Dilue in a blanket, and cradling her in my arms, we headed downriver, hoping to reach Pleasant's camp before morning.

Chapter Eight

Pleasant and Emmett had rigged a comfortable camp back in the wash, the walls of which broke the force of the north wind. From the heat thrown out by the blazing fire, we were warm, and after putting ourselves around some venison and cornbread, we sat back and watched the little towhaired girl sleep. After a while, I drifted off, managing a couple of hours' sleep.

The sleet had let up when we awakened. After a cup of hot coffee, I gently waked the little girl, gave her some coffee and cornbread, and we pushed out, despite Pleasant's plea for us to stay until the storm passed.

I gestured to the southeast. "A few hours out there are an old man, a young woman, and three more girls like this one, Pleasant." Hooking my thumb at Joe

Two-Fingers, I added, "The two of us, we're all they got. Soon as we get them safe, I plan on joining up with you and General Sam. But I got to go, Pleasant. You understand that?"

He grinned, that crooked grin that seemed to be a trait of the McAnellas. "You bet. You be careful."

"You got more girls like this one?"

I looked around at the slow, deliberate voice of Rides-With-Rain. "Yeah." I held up three fingers. "This many more. Three."

He studied Dilue for several seconds, then rose from where he squatted beside the fire. He pulled his buffalo robe around his shoulders and faced Pleasant. "I go with this one and the crazy man."

Pleasant simply nodded. I figured he knew arguing with the Cherokee chief would do no good. I'd never been around too many Indians, but those I had, they were like all of us, some bad, but mostly good. And like many white men, there were some who, once they made up their minds, would die before changing them.

Beneath the thick canopy of oak and elm leaves, we didn't pay much attention to the sleet and drizzle. Upon reaching the edge of the tallgrass prairie, I pulled up and stared out across the prairie. I'd seen ice before, but now the ice had enclosed each stem of grass in an icy cocoon, which quickly grew too heavy for the slender stem to support.

The vast tallgrass prairie which just the day before had waved in the north breeze now lay in piles and heaps, just as if a farmer with his scythe had passed through, knocking everything to the ground.

Joe Two-Fingers didn't hesitate. He rode ahead, the hooves of his sorrel shattering the ice and sending shards flying into the cold air. I fell in behind and Rides-with-Rain brought up the rear.

Around noon, the ice storm moved on past, but the heavy clouds remained. Mid-afternoon, Rides-with-Rain rode off without a word. I pulled up beside Joe. "What's he up to?"

Joe shrugged. "Beats me. Could be he just got tired of our company. Could be he decided to go home to East Texas."

I fell back behind Joe and watched until the Cherokee disappeared over the horizon. I felt Dilue squirm. I looked down at the small girl in front of me. "How you doing?"

She nodded. "Fine, Mr. Walker." She snuggled against my chest. A feeling of warmth spread through my body.

We reached the cart a hour or so before dark. To my surprise, Kate and Ned had put together a snug three-sided shelter. A cheery fire blazed in front of the open side, filling the tent with warmth.

Dilue and her little friends hugged and laughed and giggled while Joe and me squatted by the fire and told

Ned and Kate of our adventures of the last couple of days, including Joe's crazy-man act.

When the girls heard about him eating dirt, they clasped their hands over their mouths and simultaneously groaned. Dilue nodded emphatically. "He did. I saw him."

"And he rode backward on his horse too?" Mary Rusk's eyes were with disbelief.

Dilue nodded again. "Yes."

Just before we finished, a pinto pulled up beside the fire. We looked out to see a deer fall to the ground, and Rides-With-Rain step down. The girls gasped and ran behind Kate who stared up at the stately Cherokee chief in surprise. He carried his long rifle in one hand and from the other dangled a bulging parfleche bag.

Rising, I introduced the chief to them all, explaining his part in rescuing Dilue. Kate rose and went to the tall warrior. She extended her hand. "Thank you for saving the girl, Chief. I'm grateful, and her pa and ma will be very grateful."

He grunted and handed her the bag. Tentatively, she took it.

"Honey." He gestured to the girls. "Good for child. Much honey." He leaned his rifle against the tent wall and shucked his knife and bent over the deer. "Little ones need much food in bad weather."

With a grateful gleam in her eyes, Kate smiled at me, and I smiled back, at the same time pulling my knife and giving Rides-With-Rain a hand at butchering the deer.

For a batch of ragtag Texans, we sure ate well that night. Hot spoon bread dipped in honey and broiled venison dipped in honey filled our stomachs, and honey and boiled water made us a hot drink that warmed our blood.

Once or twice, I thought I spotted a trace of a smile on Rides-With-Rain's somber face as he watched the girls put away the grub.

When we awakened the next morning, four leering Santanista cavalrymen were sitting astride their war-horses staring down at us. The clouds had moved past, and the early morning sun reflected off the shiny hardware decorating their bright red blazers. On their heads, they wore flat-brimmed black hats with rounded crowns.

I started to reach for my long rifle, then decided against it. A smooth voice broke the silence of the icy morning. "Ah, *Señor*. Perhaps you should have tried. We are going . . . ah, *para matarlo sin embargo*. As you Anglos say, 'to kill you anyway.' "

His calm announcement drew sneering laughter from the five privates behind him. Joe Two-Fingers remained motionless, his eyes closed as if still sleeping, but I could see a faint movement under his soogan, and I knew he had pulled one of his belt pistols.

I fixed my eyes on the sergeant. "I did not think the Santa Anna gained his honor by murdering children and women."

The sneers vanished from their faces. The sergeant's eyes blazed. He jerked his long rifle to his shoulder and froze. His eyes grew wide, surprised. His fingers relaxed, and the rifle fell to the ground. He tried to swivel his head and look over his shoulder.

That's when I saw the arrow in his back.

The other Santanistas, stunned by the suddenness of his death, gaped at the sergeant as he tumbled to the ground. The roar of our belt pistols snapped them out of their muddled confusion.

The impact of the .50 balls knocked two from their saddles. The other three spun their horses, tangling their reins. Screams of *Carrera! Carrera!*—Run, Run—echoed above the roar of gunfire. Another cavalryman was struck by an arrow and tumbled from the saddle.

For long seconds, pandemonium prevailed in the camp. Smoke billowing from pistols, men shouting, horses whinnying, girls screaming, and finally, from the thick smoke, two Santanista cavalrymen roared, their horses in full gallop, heading west.

We pulled out immediately, now a small army ourselves, but I didn't fool myself that we could even begin to handle the patrol Santa Anna would send back after us. Maybe even two patrols, close to thirty men.

Maintaining a brisk pace, at least as brisk as you can get when you're behind a double yoke of oxen, we headed for the next river. I guessed the Lavaca, but I wasn't that familiar with the lay of the land this close to the Texas coast.

Each morning for the next three days, Rides-With-Rain disappeared, leaving Joe, Kate, and me to cast out for Santanistas or Comanche, but each evening the Cherokee chieftain rode in with prairie hens or rabbits or quail.

On the fourth day, we reached the river and crossed without incident. The prairies were still muddy, but the rivers had fallen quickly. I crossed my fingers that we would get no more rain. We pulled into a thicket of elm and pecan and set about making camp.

Rides-With-Rain rode in minutes later, handed Ned a brace of rabbits, then pointed to the west. "I go. Find soldiers. You go to Sabine," he said, gesturing to the east. "I come back."

Without another word, he plunged his pinto back into the river and swam to the western shore, where he disappeared into the underbrush lining the river.

Day after day, sunshine, rain, sleet, we lumbered east, breaking our trail as we went, all the while keeping a worried look over our shoulders.

Kate pulled up beside me just before we took a noon

break on the third day from the Lavaca River. "Do you really think the Santanistas will come after us, Bob?"

The sky was clear. The rain from the night before had washed the countryside clean. It seemed as if you could see for miles and miles. I studied our backtrail. Empty. Far to the north, Joe Two-Fingers ambled along, slow and lazy. "Beats me, Miss Kate. I reckon it depends on what kind of resistance they've run up against back there. Could be some of our folk laid back to slow Santa Anna's boys down."

Ahead, the rickety cart bounced over thick knots of roots and squished down into the mud. For several minutes, we rode side by side, neither saying a word.

Finally, she spoke up. "Why did Rides-With-Rain come with us? Did he tell you anything?"

"Nope." I kept my eyes moving, quartering the prairie around us. "He wasn't interested at first, when Joe and me rode in. But when I mentioned the Comanche had stolen a little girl, well, that's when he decided to pitch in and give us a hand."

"Hmmm," she muttered thoughtfully.

"After all," I added, grasping at reasons myself, "he's Cherokee. They been pretty much used to the white man for some time now. Not like the Apache or Comanche. Sure not like the old Karankawa."

"Makes you wonder why he decided to help after you told him about Dilue, doesn't it?"

I chuckled. "The truth is, Joe and me were so grateful for the help we didn't ask questions."

We both lapsed back into silence. I was more concerned about Santanistas than Rides-With-Rain's motives.

Strange, I told myself. We'd been traveling several days without seeing another Texan. You'd figure with all the folks that should be trying to escape ahead of Santa Anna, we'd have run into some others. Unless, I reminded myself, we were bringing up the tail end. And if that was the case, if the Santanistas did hit us, we could expect no help.

At the Colorado, we camped in a thick growth of pecan trees and berry vines. Joe rode north, and I rode south, each searching for a safe crossing. "I'm not anxious to spend two or three days building a raft," I said. "Look up that way a couple of hours, and then head back. Maybe we'll find a proper crossing."

I left Ned and Kate setting up camp. If we couldn't find a crossing, we'd have to work through the night building a raft. We did not have the luxury of time.

Dusk crept over the river bottom. I figured I'd covered ten or so miles when I turned back. Despite the flood crest having passed, there were no crossings that could be made without a raft. "Come on, boy. Let's go back," I muttered, easing the large bay around. "Maybe Joe had better luck."

The night was as black as the inside of a crow when I reached camp. Carrying on his continuous conversation with Winnie, Joe Two-Fingers was squatting in front of the fire sipping a cup of coffee when I rode up. Head wagging back and forth, he grinned crookedly and rose to his feet. "You're late, partner. I been back here a good spell." Behind him, Kate, Ned, and the girls sat cross-legged, worrying at strips of broiled venison.

The vigor in his voice caused my hopes to soar. "You found a crossing." It was a statement, not a question.

"Yep." He tilted his head back, indicating north. "About a mile. Bank's washed out fair deep. Gravel bed on one shore. The deep channel is only about fifty yards wide. We can use the ropes to pull the cart across. Current ain't all that swift."

A wave of relief flooded over me. "All right. We'll go first thing in the morning."

I swung down, put up the bay, and just as I squatted by the fire, Rides-With-Rain galloped in. He reined his pinto around. The excited animal reared and pawed at the air as the chief pointed to the west. "They come. The Mexican army. We go."

Jumping to my feet, I peered through the heavy forest of pecan and oak. "How far?"

The stoic chief held up a single finger. "One hour, maybe two."

Joe stared at me, for once forgetting about Winnie.

Ned rose and gathered the soogans. "They be that close, then we got to go now."

I kept my eyes on Joe. "What about it? Can we make the crossing at night?"

He glanced at Winnie, then arched an eyebrow at me. "I don't reckon we got no choice, do we?"

Kate chuckled and answered for all of us. "No, sir, I don't reckon we do."

Chapter Nine

Luck smiled on us. As we pulled up camp, the cloud cover broke, the stars casting a bluish glow across the river bottom. Joe Two-Fingers led the way. Kate rode beside the cart, soothing the girls' fears. Rides-With-Rain and I brought up the rear.

An hour's travel for Joe's sorrel was almost three for the oxen. Finally, we reached the wash. Below, the gravel bed gleamed in the starlight. Skillfully, Ned eased the lumbering oxen down the wash, pulling up at the edge of the river.

We pulled the girls off the cart, and untied the single horse we still trailed. I gave the reins to Kate.

Joe and Rides-With-Rain tied lariats to the wagon tongue, and I lashed mine to the left wheel. The plan was for them to swim the river, then pull the cart across. I would remain on shore, keeping the rope taut so the current wouldn't push the cart down river.

Once the cart was safely over, we'd come back, and each of us would take one of the girls across on horseback.

When we were ready, I turned to Ned, who was perched on the seat, his feet braced against the foot-board, and the fingers of his good hand holding the reins gently. "Ready, Ned?"

He grinned at me. His brilliant white teeth shone like a lantern in the darkness. "Yessir, Mr. Bob. Old Ned, he's ready."

I whistled, and Joe and Rides-With-Rain urged their ponies into the black current, playing out rope behind them. I glanced down at Kate who stood on the shore. "Here we go."

Within minutes, they emerged from dark waters onto the gravel bed. Backing their ponies, they took the slack from the rope. Joe called out. "Ready here."

Ned nodded, keeping his eyes on the oxen.

"Take it away," I shouted.

With a shrill whistle, Ned popped the reins, and the oxen stepped into the river. The force of the current hitting the cart vibrated up the rope dallied around the saddle horn. I felt my horse stiffen, then pull back against the strain forcing him toward the water.

Slowly, I played out the rope as the two across the river continued backing away, pulling the oxen and cart forward. I kept expecting trouble, but five minutes later, the cart rattled onto the gravel bed.

Joe and Rides-With-Rain swam their horses back across the river, and within minutes, we had the children across, perched on the cart, and headed for the Brazos River.

We traveled all night. None of us were familiar with this part of the state. Had we been, then we would have known what lay ahead, but as it was, we stumbled onto the swamp without warning.

Even then, we could have backtracked a few miles, turned north, and skirted the swamp, but Rides-With-Rain galloped up, and with him, any hope of skirting the swamp was lost. "They come. Soldiers. They follow trail."

Ned and I exchanged looks. Joe Two-Fingers made a slicing cut with his hand at the forbidding shadows of the swamp. "Ain't no choice now, Hoss. We got to go through the swamp."

I looked at Kate. She smiled gamely, but I could see the fear in her eyes.

Before us, the swamp lay silent and forbidding. Great trees from which Spanish moss dangled like hanging bodies cast the swamp in one dark, cold shadow. Cypress, with their drooping leaves, stood like thousands of silent ghosts, watching and waiting.

Several times in the past, I'd crossed swamps, but only when I had no choice. I never liked it. You wade through water two feet deep, maybe five, sometimes you have to swim. And you never know what is below.

More than once, I'd seen twenty-foot alligators in Texas swamps. I'd witnessed whole horses being pulled under, and then ripped to shreds when half-a-dozen hungry 'gators grabbed hold and started twisting off chunks of meat. When an alligator that that size latches onto a man, he's got no chance.

And I've seen shorelines thick with curly balls of writhing cottonmouths, a sight I'd just as soon forget.

The only advantage we had was the weather. Cold-blooded creatures both, they moved slow in the winter, preferring a deep hole out of the cold.

Looking over our backtrail, I muttered. All I saw behind us was empty prairie. "Reckon you're right." From the dull glow of the sun through the thick cloud cover, I figured it was around noon.

Because of our oxen, we moved much more slowly than the Santanistas on their well-fed, well-tended warhorses. But, once in the swamp, they could move no faster than us.

I studied our small group. "Joe and me'll take point. Try to find some ridges under water. Chief, you bring up the rear. Kate, you stay close to the wagon. I don't know how wide this swamp is, but I don't propose on slowing down until we're on the far shore."

Kate's bottom lip trembled. She nodded.

"And you girls, no screaming. Ned's got his hands full with the oxen." I dismounted, and with my bowie, chopped off a couple of limbs for clubs. I gave one to Susanna and the other to Mary Rusk. "You two are the oldest. Water moccasins try to come in the wagon, beat 'em off. You hear?"

The two girls' eyes grew wide. Mary held up the length of rawhide she used as a play whip. "I—I can use this."

I shook my head. "No. Clubs are better."

They took the clubs and nodded. "Yessir," they mumbled in unison.

For a moment, I hesitated, not wanting to frighten Kate and the girls, but at the same time, making them fully aware of the dangers we faced in the swamp. "Sometimes," I added, "snakes sun themselves in the trees. Cold, rainy weather keeps them out of the trees, but as soon as the sun comes out, they'll find a nice limb to curl up on. So, look above your heads as well as in the water, you hear?"

Kate's throat worked as she gulped. She nodded slowly. The girls' eyes turned up sharply in alarm. They whispered, "Yessir."

The water was dark brown, stained by the tannic acid from centuries of rotting hardwood leaves, the same leaves that slaves of the gentry of the time used to dye their owners' clothing.

I clicked my tongue, and my horse stepped into the water. Slowly, we made our way east in a few inches of water. The bed was firm, but I knew our luck wouldn't hold. That's the one sure thing about luck—sooner or later, it's going to change.

Despite the chill, sweat beaded on my forehead. I knew I was leading us into a journey from which there was no turning back. We were committed to the swamp, and now we would meander through it until we reached the far shore, or until . . . Well, *that* I refused to think about. One way or another, we would reach the other side.

From time to time, tiny wakes of swimming snakes broke the surface of the placid water. Once, deep in the nameless depths of the swamp, a loud splash and a squeal echoed through the shadows. The scavengers' roan tied to the cart jerked on his tie-down nervously, his eyes rolling every time a snake came near.

Joe, as always his head bobbing from side to side, rode several feet in the lead, pausing, backing, angling one direction or the other. He pulled up and looked back at me. "Water's getting deeper, Hoss."

I glanced behind, grimacing at the broad trail we were leaving. The mud we stirred in passing lay suspended in the still, stagnant water of the swamp, taking hours to sink once again to the bottom, offering an obvious trail to those following.

Maybe deeper water was what we needed. "Any kind of current, Joe?"

Joe Two-finger's sorrel stood belly deep in the dark water. He tore a leaf from a drooping cypress and tossed it in the water. He nodded. "I reckon there's a little current here."

"Good. Let's follow the current for a spell."

With a brief nod, he obliged, heading south. We followed, every set of eyes in our party carefully searching the silent swamp around and above us. Water reached the bed of the cart, soaking our gear. I half expected a howl of whining and squalling from the girls, but to my surprise, they stayed tight-lipped and calm. Susanna and Mary sat with their clubs resting on their shoulders. Jenny and Dilue kept their eyes fixed on the limbs overhead.

Kate's soft voice broke the silence of the swamp. "Where are you taking us, Bob?"

I gave a slight shrug. "Deeper water hides our tracks, and maybe the current will carry the cloudy water away before the Santanistas get here." I pointed my Kentucky rifle to the east. "I figure to cast about over there for shallow water. I'd sure like to find some dry ground for camp tonight."

Her eyes grew wide. She looked around the swamp in disbelief. "You don't mean we've got to spend the night in here?"

I reined in my bay. "We've got no idea how wide the swamp is. I've seen 'em two miles across . . . I've seen them fifty miles. We'll get out when we get out. That's all I can say."

She slumped in the saddle, her shoulders drooping in despair. She cut her eyes toward the girls who were diligently searching the dark waters surrounding them. I wasn't too worried about alligators going after the cart. If any did come out of their holes, they'd probably pay more attention to our animals' legs.

Behind us, Rides-With-Rain brought up the rear, his old eyes missing nothing. He rode the pinto as if he were part of the animal, a grace I'd noticed among the Indians, and one that few white men mastered. For hours, we slogged and splashed through three feet of water. From time to time, we stirred up a water moccasin that slithered away from us, zigzagging through the trees. Once, a small alligator paused several yards distant, its knobby eyes appearing like two chunks of wood floating on the brown water.

Time passed slowly. My thoughts wandered, my brain dulled by the steady plodding through the water. Suddenly, one of the girls screamed.

I jerked my horse around in time to see a black water moccasin hanging from a cypress limb. It dropped into the cart and instantly coiled. Mary and Susanna beat at the darting, striking head.

Kate screamed, "Bob!"

"Stay back." I yanked my pistol from my belt, but before I could fire, a three-foot arrow hummed through the air, striking the snake in the head and pinning it to the side of the cart.

The moccasin continued to squirm. All four girls had climbed up on the seat with Ned, their eyes wide as pie pans. I shucked my bowie and finished off the snake. I tossed the body into the water and handed Rides-With-Rain his arrow.

"Good shot, Chief," I said.

He grunted.

Ahead Joe Two-Fingers pulled up.

"What's wrong?" I rode forward.

"The current's turning back west. Water's starting to shallow out. I reckon that means it's time for us to turn back east."

I squinted in the direction he indicated, searching for dry land, but all I saw were countless numbers of cypress spread across an interminable expanse of water.

If we could make it through the night, we had a good chance of slipping away from the Santanistas. Come morning, our trail would be lost forever. If they continued to follow, they would do so blindly.

I looked down. The water was halfway between my horse's hocks and elbow, about midway up the forearm, maybe twenty-five, thirty inches. "Let's move. Maybe we can find some dry ground for a camp tonight."

Boosted by the hope of a dry camp, we pushed east, with Joe Two-Fingers disappearing into the swamp ahead of us. The water grew more shallow.

Our hopes soared, but just as quickly died, when Joe Two-Fingers came riding back just before twilight.

He shook his head. "Ain't nothing out there but water and more water."

By now, dusk had crept into the swamp and, like a stalking panther, lay crouched to spring. I looked back at Kate, then at Joe. With a disgusted shake of my head, I muttered, "Well, then, I reckon all we can do is push on until it's too dark, then wait till sunup to move on."

Well, now we were in one horrendous predicament, standing in the swamp all night with no fire to drive away curious animals. I'd never been in quite the same kind of pickle before. We discussed our options, of which we had none. So, we decided on our course of action for the night. The girls and Ned remained in the cart. The four of us—Kate, Joe, Rides-With-Rain, and me—would ride around the cart, like we were nighthawking a herd of cattle. With luck, our constant moving would scare off any hungry alligators or curious water moccasins, and as added insurance, we hacked off some long poles, like Indian lances to jab at any curious 'gator.

Chapter Ten

In the month of March in Texas, day and night is split about even. The sun rises somewhere around six and sets around twelve hours later, which meant we had about twelve hours of darkness and riding in a circle ahead of us. If I'd had my mustang, Horse, I wouldn't have been concerned, for I'd probably spent as much time sleeping in the saddle on his back as I had under a roof.

Our own horses' splashing in the shallow water prevented us hearing much of anything, so we stopped, one on each side of the cart. The water was only a few inches deep, so any creature moving through it would make a noise.

Kate whispered, "What do we do now?"

"We just listen," I whispered back.

As the echoes of our movements faded into the darkness, the swamp became alive. We relied on our ears, determining first that which was normal, then picking out new sounds that didn't fit the pattern.

We all heard the first alligator at the same time, a faint splash far in the darkness, drawing steadily closer. My horse tried to back up, but I held him in place. In my mind, I could see the alligator placing his feet, and I matched the splashes to his steps.

He was small, and curious. I peered into the darkness, but the shadows were too thick with the cloud cover above. The splashing suddenly stopped a few feet away. My horse stiffened, whinnying nervously. I jabbed the water with my pole, hoping to scare the 'gator. On the fourth try, I struck something that wheeled about and tore up the water in an effort to escape.

I was soaked with perspiration despite the chill of the night. I tried to relax.

Time dragged.

Three more times, alligators came close, but we were mighty lucky. They were all small.

I kept my fingers crossed that none of those monsters like I'd seen in the past would show here.

Around midnight, we got lucky. The clouds broke and a waning moon appeared, casting an eerie glow over the swamp. Without hesitation, we continued our journey.

Sunrise found us exhausted, but still moving. The

girls slept slumped against one another, still upright, their fingers still clutching the clubs. Ned sat on the seat as he had the night before, his eyes straight ahead, his good hand delicately handling the reins.

Several times, we heard the roars of alligators, but they stayed away from us. Maybe because of the commotion we made sloshing through the swamp.

We traveled all day, from time to time detouring around deep holes. Our one stroke of luck was that the clouds had passed, and we used the sun to keep our directions straight. Despite our zigzag route, we were continually moving east.

Hopefully somewhere ahead of us was dry ground.

By mid-afternoon, I was beginning to wonder if we hadn't lost ourselves in the middle of nowhere. I had no idea how far we'd traveled, but I guessed we'd been in this swamp for twenty or so miles.

Suddenly, a shout echoed through the swamp. "Over here." It was Joe Two-Fingers. I reined up and tried to pin down the direction from which the shout came. Kate pulled up beside me.

"Where is he?" She peered through the cypress.

"Can't tell." I nodded to the southeast. "I think it came from over there." I cupped my hand to my lips. "Say again," I shouted.

Seconds later came the reply. "Here. Over here. Back south."

Kate and I exchanged a hopeful look, then urged

our ponies forward, following his periodic shouts. Ned followed in the cart.

Fifteen minutes later, we rolled out of the water onto a large island thick with post oak. Several logs, long dead, lay on the shoreline, washed up by the last flood. Joe met us with a grin and waved for us to follow him. He led us to a small clearing in the middle of oak thicket in which lay the remains of old camps.

I grinned at Kate. For the first time in almost two days, we weren't sloshing through swamp water. Any other time, we'd have rested up a couple days, but as far as we knew, the Santanistas were still following.

"We have time for a fire and hot food," I said, dismounting and stretching my cramped legs. "Kate, you and Joe take care of camp. Chief, you hang around. Keep an eye out. This island is a perfect spot for sow 'gators to make their nests, though it is a mite early in the year, but you never can tell."

I looked up at the cloudless sky. "I'll drag a couple of logs up here for a fire, and then I'm backtracking for a couple of hours. See what's back there."

Kate laid her hand on my arm. "Be careful."

"Don't worry."

I took care going out, leaving what I considered an almost indiscernible trail leading back to the island. Sometimes I snapped twigs and branches, other times I punched the tip of my bowie into a cypress knee and inserted a leaf of cypress needles, leaving a trail that only the keenest-eyed Comanche could follow.

One hour out, I had found nothing except swamp and wild creatures. I turned back, noting that the sun was dropping in the west. I patted my sorrel on the neck. "Easy boy. We'll just head back like we come."

I found my marks, and as I approached the island, I felt pretty smug. We were as safe as could be expected. I planned on putting myself around some hot grub and then rolling up in my Saltillo blanket for a good night's sleep.

Approaching the island, I realized I had come in at the north end instead of the south where we'd entered earlier. I patted the sorrel. "We'll just find our way to the camp, boy. No problem."

In the moonlight, I spotted a trail and headed down it. Suddenly, my horse stumbled. I heard a whooshing sound and something struck me square across my forehead, knocking me clean off the horse and onto the ground.

"We caught somebody. Quick, Uncle Ned!" A girl's shout broke the silence following by the crashing of running feet through the underbrush. I heard Joe Two-Fingers shout, "Swing around, Chief. Let's get the jasper in the middle."

I tried to climb to my feet, but the blow had addled me. I felt a warm liquid spreading down my nose and over my lips. Blood.

"Over here," shouted one of the girls.

The running feet crashed to a halt in front of me.

Kate exclaimed. "Bob! Dear heavens, it's Bob. Susanna, you trapped Bob."

Concerned hands helped me to my feet. Joe Two-Fingers and Ned draped my arms over their shoulders and hurried me back to camp, both doing their best to keep from laughing. Joe managed to cough out, "What was you doing up here, Hoss?" He chuckled. "You shoulda come back the way you left."

I tried to reply, but I couldn't form the words. I just shook my head.

Once in camp, the women hovered over me like mama hens. Kate cleaned the small wound in my forehead; Susanna, her eyes lowered, brought me a chunk of boiled pork and slice of hot cornbread; and Mary spread my poncho and placed my saddle for a pillow.

Chief Rides-With-Rain was the only one who wasn't grinning like a chicken-eating fox, but his black eyes danced with amusement. Kate explained, "Susanna suggested we rig traps on all the trails leading in. We figured you'd come back the way you left."

I just shook my head and tried to focus my eyes on the girls who were all grouped in a huddle behind Kate. The last thing I wanted now was an argument. The blow to my forehead had muddled me. All I could say was, "Well, I reckon they worked just fine."

Ned's sonorous voice broke into my confused thoughts. "Just you sleep, Mr. Bob. We'll take care of things tonight."

He would get no dispute from me.

* * *

Next morning, my head pounded like I'd been on a three-day drunk. My eyes were swollen, but I had no idea how much until I squatted at the water's edge and looked down at the raccoon-eyed jasper staring back at me. I had a knot the size of a hen egg on my forehead and my eyes were black as midnight.

The girls made a point to stay well away from me as we ate a hasty but hot breakfast, and made ready to move out. Then, without their usual morning arguments, they assumed their positions with their clubs. I gathered the roan's reins, and when I tried to tie him to the cart, he shied away, squealing nervously and jerking his head.

"Hey," I shouted, yanking his head down. "Get down here. We don't have time for no foolishness."

Mary Rusk spoke up. "He's scared, Mr. Walker. He's scared of the snakes."

I knew he was. We all were. "I am too, Mary, but we got to go on. He'll be fine once we start." But to make sure he didn't break away, I looped a rope through his bridle and fastened him to the cart good and snug.

Almost immediately, the swamp grew deeper, reaching midway between my pony's belly and shoulders. Water lapped at the bed of the cart. The roan continued jerking against his snubbing rope.

Overhead, the skies remained clear, and a hot sun rose into the sky. "At least it isn't raining," said Kate, pulling up beside me and wrinkling her nose in a cute sort of way.

The bright sun gave me mixed feelings. Even if the water were still cold, alligators never lost the opportunity to gather the rays of the sun, often leaving their holes in the middle of the winter to soak up the heat of the sun. Fortunately, they were still lethargic for the most part, but that didn't mean they couldn't move fast when they wanted. All it meant was that in the middle of March, they weren't inclined to move fast.

During the day, we passed up one or two islands because of scaly alligators sunning on the shore, their toothy jaws gaping open, and the white of their throats a startling contrast to the black of their wet hides. And I began to notice more and more sunning snakes, some poisonous, some not.

Around noon, Kate brought us a slab of dry pork to chew on. "Cornbread got wet. Nothing but a mush now," she said, laughing.

I laughed with her. If dry pork's all we had to gnaw on, then we gnawed on dry pork.

"Any idea how much farther?" She stared into the swamp.

"No." I peered around us. As far as I could see in any direction lay swamp, miles and miles of brown water filled with thousand of cypress trees with limbs drooping like buzzards' wings. "All we can do is keep moving and hope."

It was the middle of the afternoon when the snakes

showed up. I figured it was because we'd rolled over a nest of them, but whatever the reason, an armload of them boiled up around the oxen, frightening the heavy beasts into a lumbering, stumbling charge through the swamp.

"Whoa, hey, whoa, you confounded animals!" shouted Ned, hauling back on the traces.

The snakes scattered in every direction.

The girls screamed as one tried to come over the side of the cart. We wheeled back to the cart, pulling our pistols. Noise had suddenly dropped way down on our worry list.

Susanna slammed her club on a moccasin's head, crushing it. The snake sank slowly beneath the dark water.

One sank its fangs in the shoulder of one of the oxen. The lumbering brute bellowed and shook its head, still plowing forward, blindly dragging the cart behind, bouncing it off cypress knees, tree trunks, and thick growths of swamp grass.

I rode up beside the runaway oxen. Using the wooden lance we'd probed for alligators with, I whipped it sideways along the oxen's shoulders, knocking the hissing serpent into the water.

It rose quickly, and I killed it with my belt pistol.

Ned yanked the oxen to a halt.

One of the cottonmouths struck our trailing horse in the lower jaw. The roan yanked back, snapping both the rope and reins. Squealing with fear and pain, the animal reared, lashing out with his hooves and shaking his head frantically, whipping the five-foot-long water moccasin back and forth like a bullwhip.

"Watch the cart!" I yelled.

That was our focus. Keep the snakes off the cart and away from the girls.

Pistols roared. Waterspouts erupted around the cart as lead balls ripped into snakes. The girls kept busy with their clubs. I pulled my bowie and used the twelve-inch blade like an axe.

I shot a glance at Kate on the other side of the cart. She was beating the water to a froth with her club. Something bumped my leg, and I looked around to see the white mouth of a hissing moccasin. Instantly clenching my teeth against the pain of the expected strike, I swung the bowie, and the heavy blade slashed the striking cottonmouth's gaping mouth in two. The force of my swing hurled the dead snake several feet through the air.

That's when I noticed that the sunning alligators had deserted the shoreline. A cold chill ran down my spine. Had the primeval creatures fled? Or were they edging forward, smelling the blood, hoping for a meal?

In the middle of all the shouting and firing, the roan panicked. Leaping and bounding through the four-foot deep swamp, he headed for the island with the cotton-mouth still clinging to his lower jaw.

Thirty feet from us, he hit a deep hole and started swimming.

That's when we saw the alligators.

Kate screamed. "Bob! Look!" She pointed to three wakes heading for the horse.

Joe Two-Fingers and Rides-With-Rain pulled up beside me, forming a barrier between the cart and the island. Joe and I reloaded quickly. I yelled over my shoulder, "Ned. Get those girls out of here."

He nodded and laid the straps to the oxen.

"Joe, ride ahead. Break the trail for them. The chief and me'll stay here."

The frightened squeal of the roan jerked our heads around. The animal slashed at the water as a force pulled his haunches beneath the water. Extending his neck, he lifted his head, his eyes wide with fear. In the next instant, huge jaws shot from the dark water, clamping down on his throat.

I waved Rides-With-Rain back, at the same time backing away myself. More wakes appeared, and the roan disappeared. The water was churned to a boil as alligators twisted and rolled, slapping their serrated tails against the frothing water, as they held down the unfortunate animal.

"Let's get out of here, Chief. And be as quiet as we can."

We rode in constant fear of the dark water around us and the towering trees above. The girls sat with clubs poised. Mary held her play whip, slowly waving it as a threat. I kept an eye on the oxen that had been bitten by the moccasin, but the durable creature didn't appear to be suffering any effects except a little swelling at the wound.

Life on the Texas frontier was dangerous. Daily, we lived with the knowledge that by nightfall, we could very well be lying dead, killed by a lead ball or a Comanche arrow. But very few, if any, expected to be eaten by an alligator.

Suddenly, a limber weight struck my shoulders and wrapped around my neck.

Snake!

"Yaaaa!" I shouted and grabbed at the slender body, praying I could rip it from around my neck before its fangs dug into my throat. Bracing for the pain of the strike, I tore the snake loose and hurled it as far as I could. It landed in a nearby tree.

Kate screamed. "Bob! Bob! Did he get you? Are you all right?"

My heart pounded against my chest, and I sucked in great breaths of air. I couldn't believe my luck. He hadn't struck me.

"Bob, answer me," shouted Kate, splashing through the swamp to me. "Did he bite you?"

I shook my head and froze.

Joe Two-Fingers was reaching for the snake hanging from the limb. A grin played over his rugged face and he spoke to the imaginary bird on his shoulder.

"Joe! Look out!" I shouted.

He just grinned and rode toward me, swinging the snake by the tail, or so I thought until he came close enough for me to recognize that my snake was nothing more than a four-foot length of rawhide lariat, Mary Rusk's play whip.

I jerked around and glared at the tiny girl who was staring at me through eyes the size of dinner plates. Her hands were clenched against her lips.

Kate frowned, not understanding the sudden turn of events. Then she spotted the rawhide rope in Joe's hand and burst into laughter. Joe joined in. Then Ned. Even Rides-With-Rain smiled.

But the girls weren't smiling, and neither was I.

At least for a few seconds.

Mary kept her eyes on me.

Finally, I grinned.

And we all laughed.

I rubbed my neck. "Good thing I got a sound heart. Any weaker, and it would've probably given out on me."

Mary shook her head. "I'm sorry, Mr. Walker. I was just swinging it around my head, and it slipped out of my hand. Honest."

"I understand. Don't worry about it. Just do me a favor, huh?"

"Yessir."

"Don't swing it around your head anymore. At least when I'm around. Okay? I don't think I could take another jolt like that."

Joe and Kate laughed.

And Mary nodded. “I promise.”

I slumped back in my saddle. “Then let’s get out of this swamp.”

Dilue Harris, the little towheaded girl, held her rag doll, Cassie, close to her chest. “Mr. Taylor?”

I glanced at her. “What is it, child?”

All the girls stared at me, their faces pale, their eyes wide with fear. Dilue swallowed hard. “Don’t let’s stop no more until we get out of the swamp, please.”

Ned glanced over his shoulder at the girl, then looked at me, his old eyes speaking volumes.

I forced a weak smile. “Don’t worry, Dilue. We don’t intend to. You just sit back and look after Cassie, okay?”

Slowly, she nodded.

And slowly, we continued east, hoping somewhere ahead we would reach dry ground.

An hour later, another norther blew in, dropping the temperature and hinting at rain.

Chapter Eleven

With a silly grin on my face, I peered north through the cypress trees, for the first time in my life grateful for a blue norther, which this one promised to me. Rides-With-Rain pulled up beside Kate and me. He gestured to the north. "Good. Make *gran lagarto* go."

Kate frowned up at me. "*Lagarto?*"

"Lizard. Great lizard. The alligator," I explained.

"Yeah," said Joe Two-Fingers with a grin. "Old Tough-hide." He wheeled his pony around and, head bobbing from side to side, spoke to his imaginary friend perched on his shoulder. "Let's light out, Winnie. I'd sure like to be out of this swamp before the snow."

We pushed harder, and the temperature continued

to fall. Mid-afternoon, sleet began falling. I pulled up beside the cart. "Keep those blankets tight around you, girls. It's getting colder."

As one they nodded. There was not a tear in an eye, not even from Jenny who had spent the first few days of our journey whining and crying over her lost brother. I'd never been much on praying, but right then, I said a short one for the boy.

I was proud of the girls. They'd grown up fast, and on the frontier, that's what a jasper had to do if he wanted to survive.

A shout from ahead caught my attention. Waving one of his arms over his head, Joe Two-Fingers was racing back to us, his pony's hooves spraying great fans of water with each step. My first thought was that we'd run smack-dab into Santa Anna, then I heard the word "Land."

I glanced at Kate. A faint smile erased the frown on her face and she looked at me. I nodded.

"About time," she said.

I agreed. The sleet grew heavier.

We camped in a grove of oak, stunted and warped by the prevailing winds of the Gulf of Mexico. We slept soundly that night, shielded from the elements by our tarps, and warmed by a roaring fire on the open side of our shelter.

Just before she drifted off to sleep, Kate asked, "Think we'll reach Brazoria tomorrow?"

I had no idea, but I didn't want her to worry. "Probably."

She grinned wryly and using her thumb and forefinger, tugged on the sleeve of her blue gingham dress. "I hope so. I don't care where the Mexicans are. The girls and I need to wash our clothes." A soft chuckle sounded in her throat.

I glanced down at my own clothes and nodded. "We all could use some cleaning."

Joe Two-Fingers frowned and studied his greasy black buckskins. He glanced at Winnie. "If I remember rightly, we all took a bath last summer. Ain't that right?"

He listened a moment.

All I could hear was the sleet pelting the tarp.

Joe nodded emphatically. "Yeah. That's what I thought too." He reached for his blanket and curled up next to the tent wall. "You'uns do what you want, but too much of that soap will stiffen a man's joints. Once a year is enough for anyone." And with that, he pulled the blanket up over his shoulder and immediately began snoring.

Kate and I laughed. She smiled. "Good night," she whispered.

I nodded. " 'Night."

Rides-With-Rain and I sat up a while longer, sipping coffee. On cold, dismal nights, a man drinking hot coffee beside a warm fire has plenty of time to reflect. And that's what I was doing.

I couldn't help wondering about Sam Houston and his army. Had they engaged Santa Anna already? I remembered George, my big brother. A big, gangly man always wearing a smile, he was light complexioned, and his pale skin sunburned faster than an old hen can snap up a cricket. He was always laughing. I'd come in all sour and upset, and in two minutes he would have me giggling like a schoolgirl. I couldn't believe he was gone.

He'd answered the call to go to San Antone last December. I could still see that lopsided grin of his when he looked down at me from his sorrel and made me promise to look after things. "Or I'll whop you upside the head when I get back, you hear?"

I had laughed and slapped his leg. "Any time you figure you're man enough, big brother. Any time."

Then I wondered if Ma, back in Liberty, Texas, had heard of George's death. By now, she probably had, but I wished I'd been there for her when she got the news.

A gust of wind jerked me from my reverie. I glanced at Rides-With-Rain. Curiosity got the better of me. "Tell me, Chief. How come you decided to ride with Joe and me? At the camp, you didn't seem particularly interested."

He kept his eyes fixed on the fire, as if mesmerized by the darting flames. Long seconds passed, and I figured he wasn't going to answer. Just before I reached for my blanket, he spoke, his voice a low rumble. "Comanche steal boy." He laid a finger on his chest. "My boy. We follow. We surprise at Neches River." He turned his sad eyes on me. "Boy was dead." After a few seconds, he turned his eyes back to the fire.

I guess every man has his own burden. "Sorry, Chief," I whispered. I lay down and pulled my blanket over my shoulders.

When I awakened next morning, Rides-With-Rain had disappeared. Outside, a foot of snow blanketed the ground. The sky was clear, and the sun bouncing off the snow hurt my eyes.

The girls were excited. Snow is rare in Texas, at least down in our neck of the woods. For a few moments after they awakened, the girls frolicked in the snow, shouting and laughing and throwing snowballs.

While the girls romped through the snow, Ned built the fire and put coffee on to boil. Kate sliced off some salted pork. Joe Two-Fingers grimaced at what had been our steady diet. "Sure wouldn't mind a mouthful of fresh meat." He clicked his few remaining teeth together and glanced at the invisible Winnie. "And I reckon I could manage to chew it up good too."

Suddenly, Rides-With-Rain's pinto stepped from around the corner of the tent. The chief held up three fat prairie hens. With a hoop and a holler, I grabbed them, and Kate and me plucked the feathers faster than a preacher can find a seat at the dinner table.

After we polished the hens off for breakfast, the

Cherokee chief nodded to the north. "Many deer." He pointed to the ground at his feet. "We stay here. I bring deer back. We fill our bellies. Can leave tomorrow." He rode out.

No one argued. I didn't figure the Santanistas would be marching on a day like today, and we could certainly use a day's rest. With the sun out, the snow would be gone by morning. That's when we'd begin to take up our race for the Sabine again.

Later that morning, Kate put Susanna to melting snow for hot water. She gestured to the horses. "You men go tend the animals. The girls and I need some privacy."

I eyed the quickly melting snow and realized what they had in mind. Since it was a day of rest, they figured to try to remove as much of the journey's grit and grime as possible. So, Joe and me tended the animals, gathering browse, checking hooves, and pulling out burrs in the manes and tails. The snakebit oxen showed no sign of ill effects. Even the swelling had subsided.

Afterward, we sawed some dead wood for firewood, building a more-than-ample supply for the coming night.

That evening, we feasted on juicy slabs of roasted venison, stuffing our bellies until we were ready to burst. I leaned back and patted my stomach. "I can't remember when I enjoyed a steak so much."

Kate laughed. "Three of them. I suppose you did like them."

Joe Two-Fingers groaned and spoke to Winnie. "Why'd you let me eat so much, bird?"

Dilue Harris spoke up, her voice tiny and frail. "Mr. Joe?"

He looked down at her. "What is it, girl?"

She looked at his shoulder. "Where is Winnie?" She held up her doll. "I have Cassie, but where is Winnie? You're always talking to her."

He stopped bobbing his head and studied her for several seconds. "Well, child. I'll tell you the truth. I started talking to that bird some years back to escape from a band of Cheyenne who was all set to skin me alive. You see, they were scared of crazy folk. And when they saw me talking to Winnie, they changed their minds right fast. They kill a crazy man, his spirit haunts them forever. So, I got in the habit of acting crazy, and it sorta took. Besides, sometimes it helps, talking to that ignorant bird."

Dilue's forehead wrinkled in a frown. "But how, if the bird ain't really there?"

Joe arched an eyebrow. "Maybe it is, child." He tapped a finger to the side of his head. "Maybe it is right inside my head here. Ever think about that?"

Dilue exchanged puzzled looks with the other girls, then shook her head. "No, sir. I never thought about that."

He grinned at me, then added, "Well, child. Think about it."

Jenny Adkins spoke up, the first time I'd heard a word from her in several days. "I think you're joshing us, Mr. Two-Fingers." She grinned up at Kate who returned her smile.

Joe shrugged. "Maybe I am. Maybe I ain't." He wore a big grin as he raised his arms over his head and curled his fingers into claws. "Maybe I'm just a crazy old coot who likes to bite off the heads of little girls who ask too many questions."

The girls squealed in mock terror; Ned cackled; and even Rides-With-Rain smiled. We enjoyed the evening, pushing from our minds the dangers still ahead of us.

I awakened early next morning, anxious to get traveling. In a few hours, Kate and the girls would be safe with the folks in Brazoria. Then I would be free to find Sam Houston and join up with the Texas army.

Thin patches of snow lay scattered across the prairie next morning. We pushed out with the sun, heading east for the Brazos, and with luck, Brazoria. As usual, Rides-With-Rain headed north, scouting for Santanistas.

I pulled up beside Kate. She smiled up at me. "Beautiful day," she said.

"Yeah." I cleared my throat. "We should reach Brazoria today."

She shook her head in disbelief and her smile grew wider. "Won't that be wonderful? Maybe our folks are there waiting."

I didn't let on, but I couldn't see how they could be. They might be up at Thompson's Ferry or even San Felipe, but the chances of her folks being at Brazoria were no better than the Ladies Bible Group inviting the local saloon girl to a tea-and-cookie social. "Could be. Can't tell. But what I wanted to tell you was that once we reach Brazoria, and you and the girls are safe, I'm pulling out."

She looked up at me in surprise. Disappointment etched lines across her forehead. "Pulling out? But . . . where?"

I hooked my thumb to the north. "Houston. General Houston is going to fight Santa Anna, and I want to be part of it. You remember, I told you about my brother. Well, no sawed-off little Mexican dictator is going to get away with killing a Walker. I'll get my handful of flesh before this is all over."

She smiled her understanding. "I don't blame you." She hesitated, then added, "I . . . I mean, the girls and I, we'll miss you."

I grinned at her. "Well, these last few days have been an education for me, for all of us."

Joe Two-Fingers rode in. He pointed northeast. "The Brazos is a couple miles that away." He pointed to his empty shoulder. "You can thank Winnie for our luck. There's a ferry still running."

Our hopes soared. Somehow, it all seemed fitting. Everything seemed to be falling into place right here at the end. We weren't going to be forced to swim the river, and we were going to find plenty of friends and fellow Texicans in Brazoria. And once we reached the village, I knew where I was. I had traipsed up and down the Brazos and through most of the wild countryside between the winding river and Lynch's Ferry at the mouth of the San Jacinto River. My own home was only a few days beyond the ferry.

Brazoria lay smoldering in ruins.

We halted at the edge of town, staring in stunned disbelief. A few stray dogs raced toward us, barking, skidding to a halt several feet distant. Kate mumbled, "What do you think happened? The Santanistas?"

Joe shook his head. "Hard to say. The snow washed out all the sign. Could be the Mexicans done it. Could be the people done it."

"The people?" I looked at him, puzzled. "Why would they burn their homes?"

He shrugged. "Seen it before. Once up on the Snake River, a tribe of Bannocks burned their camp when they got word a band of raiding Flatheads was coming." He gestured to the ruins. "Maybe this was the same. To keep the Santanistas from enjoying them."

Kate and I exchanged disappointed glances, hers because the village was deserted and destroyed, me because I still had my commitment to her and the girls, which meant I could not join up with General Houston.

I stared to the northeast. Lynch's Ferry was three days or so, horseback, around a hundred miles. By our mode of travel, two weeks. By now, I'd lost track of the days. I guessed it was somewhere around the first week in April, but I couldn't be sure.

And there was no telling where General Sam and his Texican army was by now. As far as I knew, he could have already met and whipped Santa Anna. Or the other way around.

"I sure the blazes hope not," I muttered, not wanting to even think about the Texicans getting whipped up on.

"What did you say?"

"Huh?" I looked around.

Kate was frowning up at me. "I thought you said something to me."

"No." I shook my head. "No."

Joe Two-Fingers spoke up. "It don't appear we're going to get no help here, so we best move on."

"You're right, Joe. I'll take point. I know the country from here on in."

We crossed the Brazos River without incident.

Before dark, Rides-With-Rain caught up with us and delivered the chilling news that the Santanista army was spread from the Brazos all the way to the

San Jacinto River to the east. "Their warriors are like the sand on the beach."

Kate gasped, and the girls began to whine.

"How far that way?" I pointed over his backtrail.

He shrugged and held up a single finger. "One sun."

Which meant we had some room to move. We had two choices. Find a spot to hole up here down south of the army, or try to slip through and reach Liberty.

So I posed the question to Kate and added, "If we stay here, and Santa Anna does whip Houston, this whole part of the country will be overrun by Santanistas. They'll find us for sure. Now, we could head for the beach and hope to flag down a passing ship."

"What are our chances of that?"

I shrugged. "Remote."

She studied me carefully, then looked at the girls thoughtfully. "You really believe we can slip past the Santanistas and reach Liberty?"

I hesitated, wanting to be sure in my own mind that I was giving her the answer that would benefit her and the girls, not me. I still wanted to get in the fight, but not at their expense. "Listen, Kate. All of us—Ned, Joe, the Chief . . . we want you safe. And with the Santanistas, we couldn't be sure. If a company with the right kind of officer takes us prisoners, we'll be treated properly, but . . ." I hesitated.

Kate spoke up. "I understand. You don't have to say any more." She set her jaw. "Let's go to Liberty."

Chapter Twelve

We camped that night on the banks of a small stream lined with a thick stand of post oak. The temperature rose well above freezing during the night as the wind shifted to the south, bringing in the warm air from off the gulf. Typical South Texas winter. Snow on the ground in the morning and a dust storm in the afternoon. Alligators hibernating one night and roaming the bayous the next.

Leaving Joe and Ned to look after Kate and the girls the next morning, I took Rides-With-Rain and headed north for a look at the Mexican army. I wanted to see where they were, what they were preparing for, and if possible, get a sense of their mood.

Stretched from Gonzales to San Jacinto, the Santanistas stood between us and the small village of Liberty.

Sooner or later, we would have to cut through their lines. And when we did, I wanted to be sure it was where they were spread the thinnest.

Riding hard the first few hours, we covered a heap of ground. Just before noon, we pulled our ponies back into a trot, a stomach-jarring gait that ate up eight or nine miles an hour.

Cut by meandering streams, the Gulf Coast prairie is as flat as a pool table, covered with tallgrass of the bluestem and cordgrass varieties, and dotted by random copses of post oak and salt cedar. The grass brushed the bellies of our ponies.

Mid-afternoon, we found a tree-lined creek running north to south. We pulled into the edge of the timber and continued, looking out over the tallgrass prairie.

Years earlier, according to my pa, the Karankawa Indians, the last of the cannibal tribes, would hide in the tallgrass, awaiting the approach of unsuspecting victims. To counter the ambush, claimed Pa, experienced travelers set fires, scorching hundreds of acres of prairie land in order to secure a safe passage.

But the Krarankawas were gone now, the last killed down on the Rio Grande by savage bands of Apaches. In the place of the Karankawas, we now had the Santanistas, determined to drive every Anglo back to the United States.

As darkness approached, we slowed our pace, preferring the night to aid our spying. Suddenly, Rides-With-Rain pulled up and pointed to the northwest.

A thin column of smoke drifted above the horizon. Soon it was joined by others. Without taking my eyes from the multiple columns, I muttered, "Looks like we found them."

He grunted.

We pulled deeper into the timber and continued north. Because the gulf coast prairie was so flat, its slow-moving creeks had more twists and bends in them than a nest of rattlesnakes.

As we rode along the creek banks, we spotted hundreds of sunning turtles, from the ancient saw-backed alligator turtles with their savage beaked jaws to the small yellow mud turtles. The tiny stream was too small for the huge alligators we found back in the swamps, although from time to time we spotted smaller ones, which was probably one of the reasons for such a great number of turtles. The other reason for their numbers was that the lazy stream formed shallow ponds of several acres, ideal turtle habitat.

One particular snapping turtle seemed to be staring at us, daring us to even pause. He was over two feet long, with three knobby ridges running the length of his brown shell. His jaws gaped open, and the sharply hooked beak glistened menacingly in the sunlight. I muttered to Rides-With-Rain, "I'd sure hate to meet up with that guy."

The chief grunted.

Just before dark, we halted. "We can ease up along the creek tonight," I suggested.

Rides-With-Rain grunted, and we dismounted.

After dark, we slipped forward on foot along the creek bank. A few minutes later, we picked out the flickering campfires through the thick tangles of grapevines and wild hackberries.

We crept closer, the thick underbrush forcing us to wade in the calf-deep creek. The banks grew apart, forming a shallow pond, on the far side of which camped the Santanistas. From where I crouched in the underbrush, I saw row after neat row of A-frame tents housing the soldiers. Nearest the creek was a row of wall tents for the officers. I counted over two hundred fires. Over a thousand men.

Rides-With-Rain headed toward the shore. I followed. I stepped on a rough rock. For a moment, the fact there were no rocks in the coastal prairie didn't register, but as soon as the rock moved, I realized I'd stepped on a snapping turtle.

About the only sensible thing I didn't do was scream, but I made enough noise running on top of the water to draw every Santanistas for miles around. I hit the shore and burrowed under tangles of barbed briars, ignoring the pain from the stickers.

Voices erupted in the camp. *"¿Cual es? ¿Lo que es ese ruido?"* Moments passed, then laughter. *"Simplemente una tortuga sacando una foto."*

Several torches left the fires, heading in my direction.

I knew enough Tex-Mex to understand their questions. What is it? What is that noise? And finally, as the torches reached the shore, one voice laughed and said, "It is just a snapping turtle. *Vea. Viene en tierra.*"

My eyes bulged. It's coming ashore? Was that what he said? *Viene en tierra.* I gulped and peered through the briars in the direction of the water. That's what he said. The turtle was coming ashore.

A few torches came my way. I pressed my face in the ground and tried not to breathe. Footsteps drew close, shuffled nearby, then slowly withdrew. In the background, soldiers were laughing and jabbering so fast I couldn't understand them.

"*Ah, caramba!*" I heard splashing in the water. Slowly, I turned my head in the direction of the noise. Peeking through the briars, I saw the retreating silhouettes of the soldiers against the fires. Two of them carried a limb between them, and on the pole dangled the alligator turtle, clinging ferociously to the wooden branch.

I studied the camp.

From the preparations, I guessed this was to be a long-term bivouac, for they had set up some semipermanent marquee tents for the officers' grub. I glanced over my shoulder to the east, wishing I knew just how far was the next contingent of Santanistas. An hour passed. The camp grew quiet.

I'd lost tract of Rides-With-Rain, but I knew he'd be waiting for me back at our horses. Slowly, clenching my teeth against the briars digging into my flesh, I wiggled backward from the vines. My only way out was as I had come, through the pond. How many more turtles were in there waiting? Luckily, I wore leather brogans. If one caught my foot, at least he couldn't take off a toe.

Taking a deep breath, I rose to a crouch and silently waded into the water, hurrying as quickly as I could without making too much of a commotion. Once or twice, I felt the water swirl around my calves as a fish or turtle swam past, but I kept moving.

Finally, I reached the shore.

I was right. Rides-With-Rain stood in the shadows next to his pinto. We mounted and headed east, planning on putting a few miles behind us before sunrise. If we didn't run across another battalion of Santanistas by then, we might have discovered the opening in their lines through which we could slip.

Twenty minutes later, my hopes crashed. Less than half-a-mile ahead of us flickered more campfires. Rides-With-Rain pulled up beside me and grunted. Making a serpentine motion with his hand, he said, "Like fish cage. Not room to escape trap."

"Yeah," I muttered, staring at the hated fires a few more seconds before turning back to our small party. We had no choice. We had to stay south of the Santanistas. Maybe later on, we would find the opening we so desperately sought.

We reached our own camp in the middle of the afternoon to find everyone, especially the girls, in a state of excitement and wonder. Even Joe Two-Fingers had stopped talking to Winnie. He'd even stopped bobbing his head.

They all started jabbering at us at the same time, and I couldn't understand a word any were saying.

"Hold it!" I shouted over the uproar. "One at a time." I looked at Ned. "What's going on here?"

He shook his head and stared out into the prairie surrounding us. "I know exactly what I saw, Mr. Bob, but sure ain't certain if I *believe* what I saw."

What in the blazes did he mean by that? I turned to Kate. "What's he talking about?"

Susanna interrupted with a shout. "A wild woman, Mr. Walker. A real, honest-to-goodness wild woman."

Jenny Adkins spoke up. "Yes, we all saw her, Mr. Walker."

The other girls nodded emphatically.

I stared at them all in disbelief. Had I not known for certain we carried no hard spirits, I'd figure somebody spiked the water. As it was, I figured instead this was some kind of practical joke.

"They swear they saw her, Bob," said Kate. "Over there just before sunrise." She pointed to the deer hanging from the limb of a tree near the water. "According to Uncle Ned, he rose early as usual to build up the fire. Susanna and Jenny were awake and went out with him. They all saw the creature gnawing on the deer. When she saw Ned and the girls, she disappeared into the prairie."

I arched an eyebrow skeptically. A wild woman? On the frontier, a man heard all sorts of rumors. I'd heard stories of wild folks out in the Trinity River bottoms, even one on the Navidad River, but usually they turned out to be runaway slaves, or Indians driven from their tribe for one reason or another.

Joe Two-Fingers conceded their claim. "Her sign's out there, Hoss. Tiny little footprints." He gestured to the south. "Followed them a good piece to the banks of a bayou. Looked up and down the shore a good piece, but she never come out."

I glanced at Rides-With-Rain, but the old Cherokee was unperturbed. At least, that's how he seemed to me. For me, no one was any harder to read than Rides-With-Rain.

Joe saw the skepticism on my face. "Come see," he said, heading for the hanging deer. "Her tracks are still in the dirt, and you can see where she chewed on the front of the haunch."

Was this some kind of joke? I looked at Kate. She read the question in my eyes and shook her head. "It's the truth, Bob. Go see."

As one, our little party went over to the hanging deer. One glance was all it took. There were the tracks, tiny things maybe six, seven inches long. And chunks of venison had been ripped from the haunch.

Kate stood at my shoulder. Her voice trembled. "Who can she be, Bob? What if she comes back?"

I looked around to Uncle Ned. "You didn't hear the horses or nothing? A stranger coming in to camp, they should have gotten spooky."

He shook his head. "No, sir. The only reason I looked at the deer was that one of the horses, Miss Kate's black, was a-looking at it. The other horses, they was sleeping with their heads down."

Joe stared at me, an eyebrow set in a questioning arch. "I ain't worried about what she might do to us, Hoss. I just don't cotton to the idea of a small woman like that running around out here all by herself."

I studied her tracks. Her first few strides after she had been discovered were almost six feet apart, an unbelievable distance given the size of her foot.

"Take a good look at those tracks, Hoss," said Joe. "You too, Chief. There's something mighty puzzling about them."

Instantly Rides-With-Rain grunted, spotting the reason behind Joe's remark. Then I spotted it. Usually, when a man takes off running, making long strides, his heel strikes the ground first. Not her. She ran on the balls of her feet, making long strides in a leaping, bounding motion like an antelope.

Kate squeezed my arm. "What are you looking at, Bob?" She studied the ground, unseeing.

I looked over my shoulder. "Let's us go on back to the fire. I need a good shot of hot coffee."

We discussed the wild woman over mugs of steaming coffee.

"She was only wearing rags, and she had long hair, Mr. Walker," said Jenny.

Uncle Ned agreed. "I woulda thought it was a wild animal until she looked around at me." He nodded emphatically, his eyes cutting again and again to the hanging deer as if expecting to see the wild woman suddenly reappear. "It was a woman. Her hair hung down almost to her knees."

Squatting by the fire and cupping the mug of steaming coffee with both hands, I told them some of the stories I'd heard as a boy. "Our village was near the Trinity River, over past San Jacinto. The river bottoms are wild and dangerous. No one has ever explored them all. One night, an old boy from Bastrop spent the night with us. He told us about a wild woman on the Navidad River, and how they tried to catch her, but all they ever saw was a shadow that almost instantly evaporated. He claimed when last they seen her, she was headed east."

"Did you . . . you ever see her?" The girls stood behind Kate, staring at me with eyes the size of washtubs.

"Nope." I half grinned. "Never did. Oh, we'd hear about runaway slaves or Indians." I shook my head.

"But I never did see any real live wild woman, or man."

With a tender expression of concern on her face, Kate stared in the direction the wild woman had disappeared. "We can't just leave her here."

For a moment, I didn't understand just what she was saying. I glanced at Joe Two-Fingers. When he arched an eyebrow, I realized her intent. I shook my head. "Oh, no. We can't hang around here." Nodding to the north, I continued, "The chief and me spotted at least six or eight companies, maybe even a battalion of Santanistas. They could be down here tomorrow. The only chance we have is to start moving and keep moving." I glanced at the setting sun. "I hate to even spend the night here, but we got to. We can't afford to waste any daylight looking for her."

Kate snugged her shawl over her shoulders. "I don't think it's ever a waste of time to go to the aid of a poor, helpless creature."

Chapter Thirteen

Evening shadows stippled across our camp as Kate stood ramrod straight and stared me square in the eyes. "Do you believe it is a waste of time?"

Joe Two-Fingers coughed nervously. Chief Rides-With-Rain stood mute. I looked at Ned who shook his head briefly. The girls watched expectantly. "What do you want to do, Miss Kate? You want us to drag our carcasses around here until the Santanistas catch us? And all because of some wild woman out there?"

"We don't know she's wild. She could have just been frightened of us." The expression on her face was sufficient evidence that she didn't believe her own words.

I studied her several seconds, admiring the set of her jaw and the fire of determination in her eyes. I supposed then that was why the good Lord provided us hard-headed men with helpmates who were compassionate and understanding. To sort of balance out the man's cussedness.

Still, I was sort of like the possum caught in the henhouse. The smart move for him was to get out, but the hens were too much of a temptation. We needed to get out, but I couldn't ignore Kate's plea. I suppose, like the possum, I'd see how close I could cut it.

"Okay, but on my terms."

She eyed me suspiciously. "Which are?"

I cut my eyes at Joe Two-Fingers who was doing his best, but failing miserably, to suppress a grin.

"We'll try tonight." I paused. She parted her lips to argue, so I continued, "Until tomorrow noon. That's the latest." I nodded to the girls. "You and the girls are more important to me than some wild woman."

Her eyes hardened, then slowly softened. "I understand. Noon tomorrow, then."

We ate a quick supper, then bedded down. The moon shone brightly, lighting the prairie with a soft light. Just before midnight, one by one, Joe, Rides-With-Rain, and I slipped into the waist-high grass on our hands and knees, each to a pre-designated spot surrounding the hanging deer. Joe took the west quadrant, the chief the east, and I went to the south. Uncle Ned kept watch on the north side. When he spotted the woman, he would signal. If, I reminded myself, she decided to come back. Wild creatures, once startled, seldom return until an extended period of time has elapsed.

Still, because of Kate, we were going to give it a shot.

The night was silent and cold. From time to time, the shuffling of a rabbit browsing broke the silence. I heard the grunting of wild hogs, then a sudden snort as something startled them. I followed their rapid progress as they raced through the tallgrass prairie.

Weary, I lay on the ground and stared up at the phalanx of stars. I must've dozed, for something jerked me awake. Unmoving, I listened carefully, but all I heard was the soft wind murmuring across the tips of the grass.

From the position of the moon, I guessed I had slept a couple or three hours. Still three hours or so until sunrise. Why had I awakened? Had I heard a sound? Or was it simply the internal clock set by a sense of wariness?

I relaxed. My thoughts drifted, as I wondered about Kate and the girls. What next? After the war? If Texas won, settlers would return to their homes. But what if Texas lost? Nowhere in the state would an Anglo be safe. Thousands of displaced Texicans would be pouring into Louisiana.

No. I pushed the thought from my head. Texas could not lose. General Sam Houston was leading the army, and if a man lived who could defeat Santa Anna, that arrogant little self-proclaimed Napoleon of the West, that man was Sam Houston.

To the east, false dawn lit the horizon, bringing a harsher, brighter light across the prairie. Suddenly, a shrill whistle rent the air.

Ned's signal!

I jerked upright, peering over the grass in the direction of the hanging deer.

Fifty yards distant, a darting shadow sped through the grass, almost like a wispy, evasive phantom. Was it just my imagination? Or the woman? Off to my left, Joe shouted and raced toward the deer. Rides-With-Rain did the same, both headed for the darting shadow.

Like a will-o'-the-wisp, it headed straight toward me. I stayed crouched, waiting until the last second to leap up and grab her.

Her speed stunned me. One second, she was fifty yards across the prairie. Two seconds later, she stood stock-still five feet from me, staring up in my eyes. My fleeting look saw she was covered with rags and had long hair. Her eyes were black, and wide with fright. The next second, before I could catch a breath, she zipped past.

By the time I spun, she was thirty yards away. I broke into a run after her. Behind me, I heard Joe and Rides-With-Rain. Another five seconds and she disappeared into the grass.

But she had made a critical mistake. She had run onto a finger of prairie some hundred feet wide surrounded on three sides by bayous. I motioned to my left. "Joe, Chief. Over there. Cut her off." The way I had it figured, we would seal off her only land exit. If she went into the water, we'd spot her.

Ned and Kate, followed by the girls, rushed up behind us. I spread them across the narrow point of land. "We got her trapped back there," I said. "Now we'll find out about this wild woman."

As usual, I was wrong.

The wild woman had vanished.

We searched the finger of prairie and found no trace of her. The only tracks were those she made when she stopped in front of me. All we found along her trails were smudges in the dust, smudges that could have come from birds dusting themselves or an animal pausing to scratch an itch, or from her.

We heard no splashing, spotted no muddy water, no footprints along the shoreline.

Kate looked up at me. "It's impossible. She couldn't have vanished so completely."

Rides-With-Rain grunted. "She is wild. The gods protect her."

I frowned at him. Joe explained, "Indians believe their gods give wild creatures . . ." He hesitated, searching for the right word. "Can make wild creatures invisible to protect them from hurt."

"Invisible?" I scoffed. "That's mighty hard to believe, Joe."

He chuckled. His eyes glittered in amusement. He looked at Winnie. "You ask him, Winnie. Ask him if it's impossible, then just where did she go?"

I shrugged. "You got me there." But I still didn't believe the invisible part. On the other hand, I'd had plenty of experience with wild creatures faking injury, then disappearing by the time I reached the spot at which they had fallen. I looked over the tiny peninsula. I figured that's what happened here. And I wouldn't have been the least surprised if she were watching us at that very moment.

Kate spoke up. "Well, we did what we could. I guess it's time to go."

I agreed.

Ned cut the rope holding the deer. I stopped him just before he loaded the carcass in the cart. "Leave it here, Ned." I looked around us. "Leave it for her."

Kate smiled, and I'll swear I saw a glimmer of sunlight on a tear in her eyes. Her voice broke. She hugged Susanna to her as she gazed wistfully across the finger of land on which we stood. "I feel so, so sorry for her."

Game was abundant, which was fortunate for we had used the last of our bacon a few days before. That night we dined on roasted turkey that Rides-With-Rain had shot in a small thicket of post oak. There was not a one of us who wouldn't have given up our portion of the turkey for a single bite of fat. Wild game is lean, without more than a trace of fat. And without some fat, a man turns into nothing more than a tough strip of leather himself.

Before turning in, I pointed out the Big Dipper, indicating our course, about forty-five degrees, which was northeast. "That should bring us out near the mouth of the San Jacinto River, east of Harrisburg," I explained.

We pulled out before sunrise next morning. I rode point by a couple miles, indicating Rides-With-Rain to do the same back to the north. Joe Two-Fingers remained with Kate and the others.

The morning was warm, almost sixty degrees. Astride the big Mexican warhorse, I cast back and forth from horizon to horizon, keeping a wary eye for Comanches or Santanistas. All that lay before me was the waving strands of thick grass. Clouds began rolling in just before noon, but brought no precipitation.

I kept thinking about the wild woman, and I couldn't help admiring Kate's desire to help the poor creature. Even though she had her hands full with the girls, she still had time to take on more problems.

Glancing over my shoulder in the direction of the cart, I wondered what would happen if I showed up at her folks' place after all this was over.

For a few minutes, I let my mind wander, but a

rabbit exploding from under my horse's feet jerked me back to the present.

Suddenly, gunshots echoed across the prairie from the direction of the cart. I counted two, three, then five or six more, one almost on top of the other. Eight, maybe nine altogether.

My blood ran cold. Wheeling my warhorse around, I dug my heels into his flanks, driving him into a gallop. Crazy, mixed-up thoughts tumbled through my brain, searching for an explanation other than the one most obvious.

Santanistas!

About halfway to the cart, I came upon a narrow bayou meandering across the prairie. Dismounting, I tied my horse in the shallow depression down which the small stream ran, and which to my good luck was just deep enough to hide him from any curious stares roving across the flat prairie.

Suddenly, I heard hoofbeats. I crouched below the top of the grass and waited, my finger resting lightly on the trigger of my Kentucky long rifle. Moments later, Joe Two-Fingers's sorrel with an empty saddle leaped the narrow bayou and disappeared into the tall grass. Back east, I heard more hoofbeats.

Slowly, I lifted my head and peered above the grass, and got a faceful of galloping horse. The horse and rider were as surprised to see me as I was them. I leaped aside and the horse veered sharply, but the Santanista cavalryman kept going straight, head over heels.

He hit on the edge of the bayou and lay still, his head bent at an unnatural angle. I winced, feeling sorry for the dead man despite the fact he was my enemy.

I spun around, searching the empty prairie before me, searching for any more approaching riders. There were none. At least not now. Certainly, when the Mexican soldier failed to return, searchers would be sent out. That was the next logical move.

Puzzling over what might have happened, I decided to take a chance. Mounting my own warhorse, I picked up the reins on the dead man's pony and headed west, slowly. The decision wasn't smart, but at the same time, if there were any more Santanistas out there, I'd spot them at the same time they spied me.

Then we'd have a horse race.

But to my surprise, all I saw was waving grass.

I rode slowly, my gaze quartering the vastness surrounding me. As a youngster, I'd been taught to gaze, not stare. A jasper stares, he focuses on an object and can easily be blindsided by another. When Pa started taking me hunting, he insisted I gaze, which enabled me to use my peripheral vision, see from the corner of my eyes. With practice, an hombre can pick up movement all the way from his left hand to his right.

And that's how I came to spot Joe Two-Fingers sprawled in the grass.

Chapter Fourteen

A north wind blew across the prairie. I could trace each gust as it raced over the grass, like giant footsteps. From the corner of my eye, I spotted grass moving against the wind.

And on the ground lay Joe Two-Fingers, facedown, a bloody hole in his left shoulder.

He moaned, and I dismounted, first searching the surrounding prairie for any Santanistas. I rolled Joe over. A lead slug had gouged out an ugly red furrow along his temple. He blinked open his eyes. I held a water jug to his cracked lips, and he drank greedily.

When he finished, I asked, "What happened, Joe?"

He coughed. "Soldiers. Santanistas. Just come up out of the grass. Bushwhacked me from the back. My horse run away, and I fell off."

I stiffened. “Kate. What about Kate and the girls? They hurt?”

“D-don’t know. It happened too fast.”

Hoofbeats sounded across the prairie. I grabbed my long rifle and threw it to my shoulder, cocking the hammer in the same motion.

I relaxed when I recognized Rides-With-Rain.

Joe Two-Fingers was tough as a mesquite post. While I patched him up, Rides-With-Rain told us what had taken place.

He was returning from scouting the Santanista army when he spotted the small patrol. Tying his pony in a shallow pool of water, he’d then hidden in the grass and watched from a distance as five Santanistas captured Kate and Uncle Ned along with the girls. They marched the small group north.

“To meet up with the rest of the army,” I muttered, desperately searching for some way to rescue them.

Rides-With-Rain shook his head. “Army far. Not reach until one sun.”

Suddenly optimistic, I looked up as I finished bandaging Joe’s shoulder. “You mean tomorrow? They won’t reach the rest of their force until tomorrow?”

“Yes.” He gave me a faint grin.

I nodded in the direction the soldiers had taken Kate and the girls. “How far?”

“We find them tonight.”

“What about the rest of the army? Which way are they headed?”

"In the rising sun."

I grimaced.

Joe struggled to his feet. With his good hand, he rummaged in his parfleche bag and pulled out a small button of mescal. "I reckon this ought to do the trick, don't you, Winnie?" He popped the clove in his mouth. From experience, I knew that within minutes, the anesthetic effect of the medicine would ease the pain in his shoulder and head.

Seeing he was still wobbly, Rides-With-Rain and I helped Joe into the saddle of the Mexican war pony I had confiscated from the dead soldier.

Our plan was simple. Stay out of sight until after dark.

The north wind continued, dropping the temperature. I kept expecting to see clouds roll in, but the sky remained clear and the air grew crisp, giving the blanket of stars overhead the brilliant sparkle of fancy crystal.

According to the Big Dipper, it was almost midnight when we spotted the campfire. Joe and I laid back while Rides-With-Rain slipped in and scouted the camp.

He returned an hour later with word that all were sleeping except for one sentry. He pulled out his knife and pointed to his chest, indicating he was the one to take out the sentry. I'd get the drop on the other four. At our signal, Joe would bring up the ponies.

"We'll take the soldiers' horses," I whispered. "The cart is too slow."

"What about the girls? Can they ride?"

I looked at Joe. "They're Texans. I reckon they rode before they walked."

We ducked into the tallgrass, leaving Joe behind. As we drew close to the small fire, Rides-With-Rain pointed east, indicating I come in from that side while he came in from the west. I checked my rifle and belt pistols.

The grass brushed against my mackinaw, and though I knew better, it sounded to my ears like brogans stomping across a puncheoned plank floor.

I spotted a lone sentry standing by the fire, staring hypnotically into the dancing flames. I slithered on my belly closer to the camp. When I had drawn as near as I dared, I paused to double-check my belt pistols once again.

As I watched, the sentry stiffened, then cut his head sharply to the west, peering into the darkness. He stood motionless, then cocked his musket and eased from the camp. Moments later, there came sounds of a faint scuffle. Rides-With-Rain warbled like a meadowlark.

Quickly, I rose and stepped into the firelight, training my rifle on the sleeping forms. Suddenly, one of the blankets erupted.

A frightened voice shouted. "*¡Despiertes!* Wake up.

¡Los Anglos estan en nosotros! The Anglos are on us."
A blossom of orange ballooned in the night, and the roar of a musket echoed in my ears.

Instinctively, I fired. A dark figure fell back, and I grabbed for my belt pistol. A heavy body struck me, knocking me back, sending the pistol flying. Grasping fingers clawed at my throat, digging into the flesh in an effort to choke off my breath.

I could smell the Santanista's rank breath. I slammed him in the side of the head with my fist, but he didn't budge.

Somewhere in the background, I heard more shots, followed by straining grunts.

I fumbled for my second belt pistol, but it was missing.

Fingers tightened around my throat. My ears roared. Brilliant spots of red exploded in my eyes. I extended my own fingers and jammed them in my attacker's eyes.

Screaming in pain, he grabbed at his eyes. I quickly rolled him on his back while he was off balance. I straddled him, trying to hold him down while I found a weapon. Off to my right, illumined by the firelight, stood Susanna Zuber, my belt pistol at her feet.

"Give me the gun!" I shouted, stretching for it.

She saw the pistol and pressed her hands to her lips. She shook her head.

"The pistol! Give it to me."

She shook her head again and backed away, her eyes fixed on mine. All I could do was gape at her.

And then the Santanista hit me right between the eyes, knocking me backward. I grabbed for my bowie knife.

Screaming in Spanish, the Santanista rolled to his knees and leaped. He landed on me, then stiffened. The firelight lit his face, and I saw his eyes open wide with surprise. He opened his lips to speak, but nothing came out.

And with a dying groan, he collapsed on top of me.

Quickly, I rolled him off me. His weight had driven the bowie through his heart. I jumped to my feet, looking for the other Santanistas, but they all lay dead.

Gun smoke lay thick over the camp. I turned to Kate. "You okay?"

She and Ned nodded.

Then I remembered Susanna. "Why the blazes didn't you give me the pistol? Couldn't you see I needed it?" I glared furiously at her.

Eyes downcast, she nodded slowly.

"Then why?" I demanded.

Sniffling, she replied, "But, Mr. Walker. Don't you remember? That night in the tent. You told me to never touch your pistols again."

Kate hugged the girl to her and glared up at me defiantly. "You can't argue that, Bob Walker. You most certainly did tell her that." A faint grin curled one side of her lips. "I heard you. We all heard you."

I wanted to stay angry, but I couldn't. They were

right. I shook my head and shrugged. "Okay, Chief. Let's get these people on horses."

He grunted and whistled.

Joe whistled back.

We turned the oxen loose and lashed our gear to our warhorses. The only item we left behind besides the cart was the empty toolbox.

Five minutes later, we were all mounted and heading east.

We made good time until a hour or so before false dawn. That's when the clouds rolled in, pouring an ocean of blackness across the prairie. Like the blind, we fumbled in the dark for blankets. Rides-With-Rain gathered the ponies' reins and lashed them together with his lariat, after which he tied the other end of the lariat around his wrist.

By sense of feel, we lay in a cluster awaiting the dawn. The wind rattled the tips of the grass above our heads. I didn't sleep. My mind was too filled with conjecture and speculation.

The Santanistas were north of us, spread from east to west according to Rides-With-Rain. But why? If Houston had met Santa Anna and defeated him, then the troops would be going west, not east. The only explanation for the army's eastward movement had to be that Santa Anna was in hot pursuit of General Houston and the Texans.

If that were true, then just how much farther could

General Houston run? We were probably just a couple days from the San Jacinto River. And what of all the other Texans fleeing Santa Anna? Had they reached safety? Or had the Napoleon of the West, as the small dictator fancied himself, captured them?

I shook my head. No. Texas couldn't go back to Mexico. Texas deserved to be a Republic. Too many men, my brother among them, had paid the price already. I wasn't too much of a book-learner, but as a youngster, I remember hearing grownups talking about the Bill of Rights, the rights of speech, religion, assembly, and the especially the right to disagree with the government. Those, explained my pa, were the undeniable, inalienable rights guaranteed every citizen in a republic.

And those words, those ideas got under my skin and stirred my pride in being a part of something greater than myself. Right now, that which was greater than me or any man was Texas.

I'd lost track of the number of days we had been running. At least two or three weeks. And the days were growing longer. I guessed we were probably somewhere around the middle of April. More than enough time had passed for a battle to have taken place.

The Gulf Coast prairie is as flat as any prairie you can imagine. Unlike many prairies where a jasper can spot another for miles, the view is misleading because of the tallgrass and cane brakes. At a mile, a man on horseback in the middle of the grass and cane is almost hidden. His silhouette and that of his pony's head can easily be mistaken for tufts of grass or clusters of cane.

For that reason, I sent Rides-With-Rain to the north, and I went northeast, leaving Joe Two-Fingers and Kate to follow. With the chief and me two or so miles ahead of the small party, we could spot trouble with enough time to plan for it.

The chief and I cast about like bird dogs sniffing out quail, stretching our reconnoitering area as much as we dared.

There was much sign of traffic crisscrossing the prairie. Once, I stumbled across a three-day-old camp where the Santanistas had bivouacked. Sitting in the saddle, I studied their trail, which moved southeast, toward the coast.

"Blast." I grimaced. That meant we were right in their middle.

Mid-afternoon, on the northernmost point of my scouting swing, I spotted Rides-With-Rain waving at me. Riding closer, I saw he was waving me to him. As I approached, he spun his pinto and rode some distance north.

I caught up with him. "What's wrong?"

He grunted and nodded. "You'll see."

Three miles north, he pulled up.

Lying in the grass was Pleasant McAnella, the brother of Robert McAnella, the messenger who rode to Fannin with me, and the one by which I sent word to Houston of Fannin's fate.

Quickly, I dismounted and lifted Pleasant's head. His eyes were sunken, his face thin, his skin drawn. A large red stain covered the belly of his buckskin shirt.

I shot a glance at Rides-With-Rain, who shook his head.

"Pleasant. Pleasant," I whispered. "Can you hear me?"

His closed eyelids twitched, then flickered open. A weak smile touched his lips. "Bob." He sucked in a shallow breath. "F-funny seeing you again. I . . ." His words faded to a whisper.

A wave of pain swept through me when I saw the bloody hole in his belly. "Don't talk, Pleasant. We'll . . ."

He coughed. "No. No. I'm gut-shot. And I'm feeling cold."

His eyes drifted shut, and he lapsed into silence.

I whispered again, "Pleasant. What about . . . what about Houston and the Texan army. Have they fought Santa Anna yet?"

After a moment, he opened his eyes. Tears spilled down his cheeks. His voice cracked in anguish. "Sam Houston's a coward."

Chapter Fifteen

I stared in disbelief at the sorrowful eyes staring up at me. Sam Houston a coward? I couldn't believe that. Not Sam Houston. I struggled to form words. "What . . . what happened, Pleasant?"

He coughed and choked on his own blood. "Houston ran. He ran . . . like a spooked coyote. We tried to get him to stand an' fight, but he never."

I looked at his belly and grimaced. "Then . . . how'd you get that hole in your belly?"

His voice grew weaker. He was dying. I could tell. His earthly body was giving up the ghost, like my Grandma would say. "Some of us . . . we run off to fight for Texas. Jumped . . . patrol. Kilt—" He groaned and strained to utter his last words. It was like the forces of life and death were battling to see who spoke the final word. "Them all," he whispered in a final gasp.

And then he just died.

I looked up at Rides-With-Rain. "Go back for the others. Bring them here while I bury him."

Without a word, he turned and rode away.

I knelt beside Pleasant and held him in my arms, and I cried.

Using my bowie, I dug out a shallow grave while Rides-With-Rain went to get the others.

Later, as I finished, I heard hoofbeats. I guessed it was the others.

Sheathing my bowie, I slowly rose, staring at the mound of fresh earth, unable to believe one of my lifelong friends lay beneath the soil.

Suddenly, a rifle roared and a slug tore up the ground at my feet.

Spinning, I reached for my belt pistols, then froze.

Leering at me from their saddles sat six of Santa Anna's elite Cuautla Cavalry Regiment. Three had their lances leveled at me, and three had their East India Pattern muskets lined up on me.

Had it not been for the three lancers, I might have made a play because of the staggering inaccuracy of their muskets, but with three steel tips aimed in my direction, I figured the law of averages was probably against me.

A corporal rode closer. He was a striking figure in

his dark blue uniform with the scarlet front. His voice was guttural. "Texan?"

While I had a fair grasp of Spanish, I played dumb. "What?" I held my hands to my side, palms up, in a gesture indicating my ignorance of his question.

He pointed his musket at me. "Texan? *Usted.*"

"Me? Texan?" Maybe I was being foolish, but I couldn't lie about Texas. On the other hand, I didn't have to tell him the truth. I placed my finger on my chest. "Me Liberty," I replied, hoping none of the Santanistas had any knowledge of Texas geography. I pointed northeast toward the small village from which I came. "Liberty."

He frowned. "No Texan?"

I jabbed my chest. "Me Liberty."

He jabbered over his shoulder to the privates behind him. Two dismounted and quickly disarmed me. The corporal motioned to my horse. "*¡Venga!*"

I hesitated, knowing that he wanted me to follow him.

He motioned to my horse and waved for me to follow. "*¡Venga!*"

As I mounted my pony, I said a short prayer, grateful that I had switched from the Santanista war pony to one I'd taken from the scavengers. There was no question in my mind that if they'd discovered I was riding one of their warhorses, I'd be back there on the ground beside Pleasant.

We rode north.

From bits and pieces of their conversation, I learned I had indeed been captured by a patrol with the Cuautla Cavalry Regiment. They were taking me to their main camp so an interpreter could question me.

While the words were never spoken, I knew my fate when the interpreter had completed questioning me. Santa Anna had already proclaimed it. Death to all Anglos!

I prayed for a heavy rainstorm to explode on us, giving me a chance to make a break. The skies remained cloudy, but no rain. I hoped we'd have to camp tonight before reaching the battalion bivouac. Maybe I could escape under cover of darkness.

But just as the sun set, we spotted the bivouac far to the north. I even prayed for a hurricane, but the wind remained strong out of the north, drying the prairie grass.

With a shrug, I figured I'd used up all the favors I had in store for me.

My hopes sank.

For a moment, I considered making a run for it, but I knew my chances were worse than those of a greenhorn gambler in a short deck game. They'd stripped me of all my weapons, and I felt as naked as a newborn mockingbird.

If it all came down to cut bait or fish, I reckoned I'd go out the best way I could.

So naturally, when we rode into the camp, I was mighty depressed. I figured I had only a handful of minutes left on this earth. I just wished I could take a few of those Santanistas out with me.

Just as we entered the camp, rough hands yanked me from my pony and shoved me forward. I jerked around, ready to pop someone between the eyes, and came face to face with the muzzle of a belt pistol two inches in front of my nose.

A leering Santanistic laughed and shoved me backward. *"!Vaya, gringo. Movimiento!"*

Guttural laughs echoed his words as I stumbled forward.

"*La tiendo*," he growled, indicating a wall tent of bleached canvas next to a larger one of the same material. The second one flew small pennants of green and red from each of the four corners of the tent. A larger pennant waved from the peak of the four-sided tent. Both had a canvas fly stretched over the open doorways. Another shove sent me tumbling to the ground at the door of the tent.

A knee jammed in my back and hands twisted my arms behind my back. At the same time, knees slammed against my legs. Rawhide cut into my wrists and ankles.

I lay motionless, knowing full well struggle was useless. All it could do was anger the Santanistas.

They didn't need angering.

A deafening explosion of curses burst from one of the soldiers, and a sharp kick slammed into my ribs.

Searing pain shot through my body. I groaned through clenched teeth and tried to curl into a ball.

Three more vicious kicks battered my lanky frame. I passed out.

I don't know how long I lay unconscious, but a faceful of cold water jerked me awake. I groaned and tried to open my eyes. My vision blurred, then cleared.

A stiff-necked Santanista officer stared down at me, his thin lips curled in distaste. His dark blue uniform with the scarlet front was clean and neat. His black boots wore a dazzling shine. Under one arm, he held his shako, the high-topped hat with the shiny black visor and gaudy plume. He nodded briefly to the corporal next to him. Two more soldiers stood in the background.

The corporal nodded deferentially. "Colonel Allende."

Colonel Allende nodded. The corporal spoke to me in halting English. "Where . . . is Sam Houston, Texan?"

I played dumb, which wasn't all that hard for me. "Sam who?"

He turned to the officer and translated my reply.

The officer glowered at me. The vein in his neck bulged.

I shook my head. "*Señor.* I know of no one by that name. I came here from California. I know no one in this country."

The corporal repeated my answer.

The officer glared at me suspiciously, then spoke brusquely. *"¡El queda!"*

"He says that you lie," said the interpreter with a smirk.

I shook my head. "No."

Quick as a stroke of lightning, the officer stepped forward and slapped me across the face. *"¡Mentiroso!"*

The corporal said. "He says you are a liar."

"No." I glared up at him. My voice trembled with anger. "I tell you the truth."

The corporal quickly translated.

Colonel Allende straightened his shoulders and arched an eyebrow.

I continued. "I am new to this country. I came from the mountains where I hunted buffalo, antelope. I go to New Orleans."

The interpreter spoke quickly.

The Santanista officer studied me through narrowed eyes for several seconds. I tried to look innocent and harmless. He shrugged his shoulders. He spoke to the corporal and the other two soldiers, then departed the tent.

I wondered if I had convinced him.

Obviously not, for the corporal turned back to me and aimed a blow at my forehead. I jerked away and fell over on my side, a perfect target for the barrage of boot heels that followed. I mercifully passed out.

* * *

I awakened to complete darkness. Had they blinded me with those kicks to the head? I drew a deep breath and sucked dust and grass into my nostrils. That's when I realized I was lying on the ground, face down.

Slowly, I turned my head to one side. My muscles screamed in pain. I could see campfires glowing against the canvas walls. Gingerly, I pulled against the rawhide binding my wrists and ankles. It refused to budge.

The beating the three Santanistas had administered to me indicated that the officer had not believed me, and if that was the case, then I could bet every last cent in my pocket he would return. And when he did, it would be with the determination to either get his information, or kill me while trying.

I considered telling him the truth, that the last time I'd seen Sam Houston was at Gonzales. And that was three or four weeks earlier. I could say that without lying for I had no idea where he was now.

But in the pit of my stomach, I knew that regardless of what I told him, one fate awaited me.

Death to all Anglos. Santa Anna's battle cry. I could expect no more.

I struggled with my bonds. If I was going to die, I might as well die trying to escape. Savagely, I twisted my wrists at sharp angles to each other, clenching my teeth against the pain of the rawhide cutting into my flesh as I attempted to stretch the tough leather.

Then I spotted the silhouette of a water jug against the canvas wall. My hopes surged.

Quickly I rolled across the floor to the clay jug. Struggling to sit up, I tried to grab the slender neck of the jug and tilt the jar so water would soak the rawhide. The jug was too heavy.

Instead, I turned it on its side. Water spilled from the mouth of the jug. Desperately, I tried to stick my wrists in the flowing water. Within seconds, the jug was empty.

I twisted and strained at the rawhide.

Slowly, my bonds began to stretch as the water soaked the leather, softening it. I worked frantically.

Little by little, the rawhide gave until finally, I slipped one wrist free.

Leaning forward, I loosened the leather binding my ankles and jumped to my feet, at the same time, searching the darkness for a weapon of some sort. All I had was the empty water jug.

I hefted it over my head and took a couple practice swings, wishing I had the snobbish Santanista captain in front of me. I couldn't resist grinning at the thought of shattering the clay pot over his head.

I hesitated. I sniffed the air. Smoke. Burning grass.

Suddenly, voices broke the silence. I pressed into the dark shadows near the entrance, at the same time raising the jug over my head. The voice grew nearer. A hand tugged the canvas door partially open, then paused as the second voice spoke.

I readied the jug, knowing full well that my chances for escape had dwindled to nothing. The soldiers hesitated before entering the tent, engrossed in earnest conversation. From the few words I could understand, Santa Anna was moving to San Jacinto to capture the newly formed Texas government. He would be reinforced by General Cos. Without the government for support, Sam Houston would capitulate.

"*¡Mirada!*" At the sharp exclamation, the hand holding the canvas door open jerked away. Moments later, running footsteps retreated from the tent.

I waited to the count of ten. Taking a deep breath, I peered outside. Smoke stung my eyes, and then in the distance, I saw a wall of fire rushing toward the bivouac.

The camp exploded into a melee of frantic shouting, ignored orders, squealing horses, and panicking soldiers. The smoke grew thicker.

I eyed the jug in my hand. It was the only weapon I had. "Let's give it a shot," I muttered, tugging my hat over my eyes and dashing into the night.

As I darted past the large wall tent flying the pennants, Colonel Allende suddenly appeared. We both jerked to a halt, surprised.

He opened his mouth to yell, but I smashed the clay jug into his temple. The sneering Santanista officer sagged to the ground without a whimper.

I grabbed his belt pistol and saber, then raced into the night. The tallgrass slapped my legs, wrapped around my ankles. I tripped and fell several times, but slowly the shouting died away behind me as the roar of the fire drew ever closer to the camp.

Without warning, a dark figure rose from the ground in front of me. I slid to a halt, at the same time jerking the saber over my head, and slashed downward with all my strength.

Chapter Sixteen

The starlight lit the figure before me dimly, but at the last second, I recognized Rides-With-Rain. I tried to halt the force of my blow, but I had committed all my energy into the swing. Instantly, I released my grip on the handle.

With the reflexes of a young brave, the elderly Cherokee dropped to his knees and whipped his musket above his head with both hands. The saber slammed into the barrel, diffusing a spray of sparks in the dark night, then whipped back over my head.

He rolled backward and leaped to his feet, still holding the musket to ward off any further blows. "Stop! I come to help," he shouted.

I held both hands over my head. "Sorry, Chief. I didn't recognize you. I just struck out."

Lowering the musket, he eyed the approaching prairie fire, the flames of which cast golden splashes across his high cheekbones. "Come. The others wait. The fire will drive the Santanistas to the north. We ride east through the night."

Three hours south of the fire, we met up with Kate and the girls. Joe Two-Fingers and Ned rode in moments later from their nightly patrol around the temporary camp. There was coffee, though the grounds had been used more than once. Still, it was hot, and I was mighty happy to be back with Kate and the girls.

I briefly told them what had taken place. "To tell the truth, I don't think that bunch of Santanistas know what's going on."

Ned spoke up. "Mr. Bob, you reckon that Santa Anna was with them what captured you?"

"No." I briefly outlined the conversation I'd overheard from inside the tent. "He's at San Jacinto, just on the other side of Harrisburg. I think this battalion is heading that way to reinforce him."

Kate studied me a moment. "If that's true, then we have Santanistas on all sides except to the south. We can't get through to Liberty."

One of the girls whimpered.

I tried to be as reassuring as I could. "Even if we have to go south, we can reach the beach and make our way along it to Sabine Pass. From there, we cross the river into Louisiana.

Chief Rides-With-Rain interrupted. "We go now." He pointed his long rifle to the east. "Sun rises soon."

With all of us on horseback, we made good time, riding hard until sunrise and then taking a short break to breathe our ponies and put ourselves around some venison and hot coffee.

I stood at the edge of our hasty camp, peering east and north.

"See anything, Hoss?" growled Joe Two-Fingers, halting at my side.

"Nope. Just that storm brewing back to the north," I added, nodding to the bank of dark clouds rolling across the horizon.

He studied them a few moments. "What month you reckon this is?"

Keeping my eyes on the clouds, I replied, "I figure April."

Joe grunted. "Seems like I remember that around the middle of April we always caught us a humdinger of a storm." He dipped his head in the direction of the approaching clouds. "I got a feeling in my bones that might be it."

I couldn't help chuckling. "We been through so many storms the last few weeks, this one would have to be the King of the Mountain to bother me."

He glanced at Winnie, the invisible Windingo on his shoulder. "What you think? We need to shelter up?" The gap-toothed old mountain man listened silently a moment, then grunted. "Yep. Me too."

Back with the others, Rides-With-Rain agreed.

Gesturing to our ponies, I said, "Then let's go find some place to shelter up."

Within a mile, we rode into a basin that appeared to be four or five miles wide. On the north side, we found a thick stand of pecan and oak in the middle of which was a small rise. I studied the country around us. It seemed familiar, but I couldn't be sure.

Stretching a tarp between two thick trees, we lashed it tightly at the top and bottom to the tree trunks. We overlapped the top to keep out the weather. We divided the shelter in half with a tarp, giving Kate and the girls some privacy.

The wind shifted before we finished, ushering in chilling drafts of frigid air. Joe and the Chief had been right. We had a storm coming that would make a jasper think that bucking the tiger was no more than drinking pond water.

The temperature plunged and we piled firewood in our side of the tent to keep it dry. Sometime after dark, a fine mist began to fall, freezing as it struck the ground.

I racked my brain, trying to remember if I'd ever been here before. If this were the place I was thinking about, there should be a narrow valley a couple of miles northeast. I stared into the night, wondering.

The reason I remembered the valley is that it was an oddity in this part of the state. Like I said earlier, the Gulf Coast prairie is flatter than a pool table. One peculiarity is that beneath the prairie, there were huge caverns, domes, my pa called them. Best folks could guess, saltwater had washed them out millions of years ago. Some of them caved in, and that's where I figured this valley came from.

We took turns staying up during the night to feed the fire, waiting expectantly for the storm to abate. At sunrise, the icy rain continued, adding layer after layer to the countryside. The roof of our tent began sagging. From inside, we struck the canvas over our heads, breaking the ice and sending it sliding to the ground.

Limbs sagged, drooped to the ground. With the report of gunshots, great branches snapped and crashed to the icy ground. And still the icy mist continued.

Late in the afternoon, Mary, Kate's sister, exclaimed, "Look!" She pointed to the basin beyond the timber. A herd of buffalo had moved into the far end of the valley, searching for graze beneath the ice that was now almost two inches thick. From the size of the herd, I guessed four or five thousand.

We had plenty of grub, so I was right tickled to put off the risky task of killing a buffalo and then the arduous labor of hauling the meat back to camp. Instead, I poured me a tin cup of steaming coffee and leaned back against my saddle.

Texas weather is as unpredictable as a wild mustang. Just before dark, the rain stopped. The wind shifted, and the temperature began rising. By midnight, we heard the first drops of water slapping on the roof of our tent. And then the ice started falling, peeling away from the limbs and trunks and splashing to the muddy ground.

I'd been in a few ice storms in the past, but I never ceased to be amazed at the amount of water contained in the ice.

Next morning, the sun rose in a clear sky. The basin south of us was a small lake. The buffalo had disappeared. We whipped up a hurried breakfast, packed our gear, and headed out, bound for Harrisburg and the ferry crossing the San Jacinto River. Twenty or so miles beyond was Liberty, and safety.

I kept thinking about the narrow valley. It was only four hours from Harrisburg.

A couple of miles from camp, we came upon the buffalo herd, grazing contented. We skirted the large beasts, not wanting to spook them into a stampede. I'd witnessed a runaway herd more than once. Nothing stood in their way. Heavy, bulky creatures over two thousand pounds, running as fast as a locomotive, they crashed over and through any obstacle in their path.

Another mile past the herd, I pulled up. "Whoopee!" I shouted, staring down into the valley I'd been waiting for.

Kate reined up, startled. The others looked at me like all my cups weren't in the cupboard. "What happened?" she exclaimed.

I laughed and explained. "I know where we are

now. See that valley? Harrisburg is four hours away. We'll be across the San Jacinto River by nighttime with any luck."

For the first time in days, a sense of relief swept over our small party. The girls giggled; Ned grinned; Rides-With-Rain grunted; Joe Two-Fingers started talking to Winnie again; and Kate smiled at me.

I returned her smile, relieved our race to safety was over, and proud we had managed to evade the Santanistics for over two hundred miles.

We rode into the narrow valley.

Halfway through, a company of the cruel Delores Cavalry ambushed us.

Chapter Seventeen

The valley was close to three miles long and a quarter-of-a-mile wide. Lances bristling, voices raised in a battle cry, the Santanista cavalry burst out of the trees on the far side of the valley in a galloping charge. The sun reflected off their warhorses' armor. We wheeled our ponies and headed for the tree-covered slopes before us. The slopes were steep, for the most part too steep for a pony except the trail up which Rides-With-Rain led us. I brought up the rear. Before we reached the top, I saw Ned stiffen in his saddle, then slump forward across his pony's neck.

We found a depression on top of the trail where we took refuge under a barrage of lead slugs. I pulled Ned from his saddle and leaned him up against a small oak.

"Where the blazes did they come from?" Joe Two-

Fingers shouted above the rifle fire as he leaped from his horse and snapped his long rifle to his shoulder.

We were too busy ducking and searching for a spot from which we could fight to answer. Kate led the ponies to the rear of the concavity and gave Jenny and Dilue the reins for the two girls to hang on for dear life. Then she hurried to me where I was tending Ned. Joe Two-Fingers and Rides-With-Rain had flopped on their bellies at the front of our bulwark, rifles at their shoulders.

"How's Ned?" Kate's face was drawn with fear.

The slug had hit the old man's left collarbone, shattering it. "He'll make it," I shouted above the racket of rifle fire. "But he ain't going anywhere any time soon."

Through clenched teeth, Ned grunted. "I'm fine, Mr. Bob." Sweat shone on his forehead. He nodded to Joe and the Chief. "Them two need you up there."

Below, half of the multihued cavalry fired up at us while the other half milled about at the base of the trail, searching for another way up the steep hills.

Once we were in position, Kate spoke up. "They must've been hiding in the trees across the valley."

"Yeah," Joe Two-Fingers muttered. "That's why we didn't spot them." He shook his head. "If that don't just boil the water. And just when we just about had got ourselves nice and safe."

A rifle ball slammed into the black soil at my shoulder. I took aim at one of the riders below and squeezed off a shot. A rider tumbled from his warhorse.

"Take your time," Joe Two-Fingers warned. "There be only four of us."

Susanna Zuber, the girl I'd warned to never lay a hand on one of my guns, touched me on the shoulder. "I can load, Mr. Walker." She looked me square in the eyes. "That is, if you don't mind me touching your gun." She nodded to Mary Rusk. "Me and Mary can load while you all shoot."

I glanced at Kate. She grinned and nodded. "Well, child. I reckon this time, the situation is a mite different." I handed Susanna the rifle, lead, and powder, then reached for one of Joe Two-Fingers's extra belt pistols. "With the girls loading, we got eight or nine shots now."

As far as distance, we had the advantage. Our long rifles were accurate at two hundred yards while their Mexican *escopetas* and the surplus British Baker rifle weren't accurate over seventy. The only problem was they outnumbered us three to one, counting the girls. And we had a wounded man who would probably die if we had to run for our lives.

Saber waving, an officer led a charge up the trail. Three well-placed lead balls knocked him and the next two cavalrymen out of their saddles. The others jammed together in an effort to retreat back down the trail, out of range of our deadly rifles.

Twice more, they made suicidal charges up the trail. Twice more, brave cavalrymen fell.

Slugs cut the air about us. We returned fire, our Kentucky long rifles strafing the disorganized cavalry in the valley. A haze of white smoke hung thick in the valley. What little breeze there was coming up the hill carried our smoke away, giving the Santanistas a clearer shot.

Steadily we aimed and fired.

By now, discouraged by our lethal fire, the soldiers had dismounted and taken refuge among the trees below, their intent obvious. If they couldn't storm us on horseback, then they would do it on foot.

I kept wondering when one of them was going to come up with the idea of flanking us, or else simply riding out of the valley and coming up from behind.

Kate gave me a worried look. "My powder's running low."

One glance at the others told me they were all paddling in the same canoe.

I glanced to the northeast, toward Harrisburg and the San Jacinto River. We were so blasted close, and yet so far. On the ground behind us, Susanna and Mary worked diligently reloading the rifles and pistols. A pitifully small mound of lead balls lay on the ground between them.

Anyway you sliced the pie, we were in trouble. Because of Ned, we couldn't run. Sooner or later, they would surround us, and when we ran out of lead and powder . . . I shook my head. I couldn't let that happen.

And then I had an idea. A wild, crazy idea that would probably get me killed. And even if I made it out of here, if I was wrong, I would probably get the others captured, or shot.

Still, our chances were dwindling. A cornered rooster facing a dozen possums had a better chance of getting out than we did.

I jammed two pistols under my belt and grabbed the reins of my horse from Dilue. Hurriedly, I explained my plan to the others.

Kate winced, her eyebrows knitted. "They'll kill you."

Joe Two-Fingers winked at Winnie. "Happens to the best of us." He chuckled.

I arched an eyebrow. "I'm going out the back way. They'll never know I'm gone." I looked at Kate. "If everything works out, I'll be back in five minutes."

"Don't worry. We'll still be here," growled the old mountain man.

Kate forced a brave smile.

Swinging into the saddle, I pointed the bay southwest, toward the herd of grazing buffalo. Digging my heels into my pony's flanks, I muttered a short prayer that our gunfire hadn't spooked them.

The great herd had grazed to within a half-mile of the valley. Though I skirted wide around the herd, several sentry bulls trotted out toward me, heads raised, tails stiff.

Behind, I heard sporadic gunfire from the valley.

I stayed wide of the animals until I reached the rear. When I spotted the valley directly across the herd from me, I pulled up. Quickly, I removed my mackinaw and pulled out a pistol.

Taking a deep breath, I fired the pistol into the air, shouted at the top of my lungs, and waved my coat frantically over my head. "Yeeee-ah!" I dashed toward the herd.

As one, the shaggy beasts spun and within ten yards had reached a wide-open gallop, heading directly for the valley. The herd strung out, but it was still a quarter-of-a-mile wide.

Just before it reached the mouth of the valley, the lead cow veered right. Slapping my coat against the bay's rump, I raced forward along the side of the galloping animals. Pulling my second pistol, I fired at the cow.

Abruptly, she cut back into the valley, leading five thousand buffalo down on the Santanista cavalry, leaving a broad trail of torn and muddy turf behind.

I dropped back to the rear, and when I reached the trail to our battlement, I jerked the bay to a halt. The ground was soggy mud. Every piece of grass had been destroyed, small trees smashed. The valley had been transformed into complete desolation by the charging buffalo.

When I dismounted, Kate jumped up from tending Ned and threw her arms around my neck. I stiffened, uncertain as to just what I should do. But, I had to admit, she sure felt good hugging my neck.

In the next second, she dropped her arms and backed away, dropping her gaze to the ground. "I'm . . . I'm sorry. It's just . . ." She looked up. "You saved our lives."

I pointed after the disappearing herd. "They saved us. At least for the time being," I added, cutting my eyes to Joe Two-Fingers and the chief. "How's Ned?"

The old man spoke up. "I'm fine, Mr. Bob. Just fine."

Kate knelt and finished dressing his wound. Slipping his arm in a sling, Kate looped a rope around his chest, snugging his upper arm to his ribs, immobilizing the collarbone. She looked up at me. "That's the best I can do."

"Can you ride, Ned? Not hard, but steady?" I asked. "Soon as those old boys reorganize themselves, they're coming after us. We need to get out of here as fast as we can."

He grinned despite the pain in his eyes. "Don't you worry none about old Ned. I'm fine." He tried to stand, but fell back. He tried again. I seized his arm and helped him to his feet.

"Hang on, Ned," I said. "Four hours is all we need. We'll be in Harrisburg by them."

Sweat beaded on his face. "Just you all help me in the saddle. I'll stay right with you."

* * *

We moved out, and every minute I expected to look over my shoulder and see the Delores Cavalry pursuing us.

Two hours later, I reined up, halting our small party. From the northeast, in the direction of Harrisburg, there came cannon fire booming across the prairie. I looked around at Kate.

"What do you suppose it is?" Her brows knit in question.

All I could figure was the Texicans and Santanistas were fighting. And we were riding straight into it. "Beats me. Maybe we best find a spot to hole up until we can scout ahead and find out just what is going on."

Joe Two-Fingers grunted. "Too late for that, Hoss. Take a look."

We looked over his shoulder.

Kate gasped. Jenny Adkins started sniffling.

On the horizon came a large number of horsemen, riding hard on our trail.

"What do you think?" It was a stupid question.

The old mountain man chuckled. "Same as you, Hoss."

The Delores Cavalry.

I gave Ned a hard look. "Grit your teeth, old man. We gotta ride now."

And ride we did, hard, but Ned slowed us. The cavalry gained steadily, but we were still out of rifle range. I figured we had another thirty minutes before we had to stand and fight.

Finally, I spied what I had been looking for. Ahead was a tree line winding across the prairie. "We'll make our stand there," I shouted above the sound of our horses. "At that creek." I planned on Joe, the chief, and me holding back the cavalry while Kate, Ned, and the girls kept on for Harrisburg.

Just as we reached the narrow creek, the big black warhorse Kate rode stumbled, sending her somersaulting head over heels. She slammed into the far bank of the creek and went limp.

Fear electrified my body, as I remembered the Santanista cavalryman who was thrown from his pony and broke his neck. I leaped from the bay and splashed through the narrow stream. "Kate!" My heart jumped up in my throat. I dropped to my knees and felt her pulse. It beat steady and strong. I sighed with relief. Quickly, I slipped my arm under her shoulders and neck, lifting her gently. She was as limp as the rag doll Dilue Harris carried with her.

"Here. Over here!" Joe Two-Fingers shouted, swinging down from his pony and kneeling behind a fallen oak on the bank of the stream.

I shot a look across the prairie. The Delores Cavalry was drawing closer.

Ned and Rides-With-Rain were herding the girls behind the windfall. Moving as gently as I could, I carried Kate's limp body up the creek and lay her on the ground behind the windfall. The girls sniffled.

Mary looked up at me. "Will . . . will my sister be all right, Mr. Walker? Huh?"

I smiled, hoping to give them the reassurance I didn't feel. "Yes, hon. She'll be just fine." I looked around, my hopes sinking. Now, with Kate unconscious, there was no way to effect the girls' escape.

We all had to stay and fight.

Chapter Eighteen

We pooled our powder and lead, a pitifully small supply of each. Joe Two-Fingers grunted and spoke to Winnie. "Well, old girl. Looks like we're up against a real grizzly this time."

Then he, along with me and Rides-With-Rain, rested his long rifles on the flaking bark of the dead tree, lining the muzzle on the approaching riders. I counted a dozen, leaning forward in the saddle with lances poised. "Boys," I drawled, "make every shot count. We ain't got that much lead to spare."

I kept trying to come up with a way out. Another buffalo stampede, or something similar. I couldn't believe this was how our race across the state was going to end. Killed out on the desolate coastal prairie. I turned to Ned who was cradling Kate in the curl of his good arm. "You stay with Kate and keep the girls with you, Ned. We'll take down what Santanistas we can. I reckon you won't be hurt none, nor will the girls. If they should turn you loose, get to Liberty. Look up my family. Tell 'em I sent you. They'll take care of you and help you get back home."

Slowly, old Ned nodded, his eyes fixed on mine. A tear glistened. "Good luck to you, Mr. Bob."

Setting my jaw, I turned back to the thundering cavalry. Counting my belt pistol, I had three shots. And there were an even dozen of the cavalrymen coming. Not very good odds. "Come on, boys," I muttered between clenched teeth. "Let's see how many of those fellers we can put on the ground."

Joe Two-Fingers looked at Winnie. "Well, old girl. Looks like its time to start the dance."

When the charging Santanistas were a hundred yards from us, we fired. Three horses jerked and three riders somersaulted backwards off their ponies, sprawling in the mud, unmoving.

Quickly, I pulled out my belt pistols. With them, I had to wait until the last second. I clenched my teeth.

Suddenly, hoofbeats sounded behind us. I jerked around to see three or four Santanista cavalrymen racing toward us. I grimaced. "Well, I reckon that just about ties the knot." But then I noticed they weren't carrying any weapons.

When they reached the creek, they didn't pause, nor did they pull up when they reached the Delores Cavalry, instead they raced through the milling cavalrymen. Moments later, I spotted more Santanista soldiers, these on foot, running in our direction as hard as they could. "What the blazes is going on?" I muttered, puzzled, but quickly reloading my muzzleloader.

We exchanged confused looks.

"Beats me," mumbled Joe Two-Fingers.

Two Santanista infantry men in their white cotton fatigue uniforms splashed across the creek. One of the Delores Cavalry stopped a soldier. After several moments of excited talk and exaggerated pointing in our direction, the small soldier took off running again. Moments later, the Delores Cavalry followed, leaving us by ourselves.

They were running, but from what?

I heard a mumble from the girls.

Kate had awakened. I felt as if a thousand-pound weight had been lifted from my shoulders.

She blinked her eyes. "Wh . . . what happened?"

"How you feeling?" My eyes searched her face.

She winced and moved her head. "Got a whopper of a headache."

We all chuckled. If she could joke, she wasn't hurt too bad.

"You took a spill."

Ned chuckled. "Yes, ma'am. Some big spill."

The crashing of underbrush interrupted us. We looked up to see a frightened Santanista soldier staring at us, momentarily frozen. And then with a scream, he leaped from the creek and raced across the prairie.

Kate struggled to sit up. "What's going on?"

I shook my head. "Can't tell. Something's happened. The Mexican fellas are running like spooked cats."

For the next several minutes, we watched in fascination as more than a dozen Santanista infantrymen stumbled past.

"I don't know about the rest of you," I said. "But I want to know what set them off."

One of the soldiers raced toward our windfall. Just before he reached the creek, I stepped from behind the oak and pointed the muzzle of my rifle at him. *"¡Alto!"*

Wide-eyed with fear, he threw up his hands and slid to a halt. Sweat rolled down his frightened face, leaving trails in the dirt that covered his swarthy cheeks. He screamed. *"¡Me no Alamo! !Me no Goliad!"* And then he dropped to his knees and buried his face in the ground. He curled his arms over his head. *"¡Me no Alamo! !Me no Goliad!"* He sobbed.

I glanced over my shoulder as the others rose to their feet. Nudging the frightened soldier with the muzzle, I told him to stand. *"¡Consiga a sus pies!"*

Shivering, his eyes bulging in fear, he slowly rose, shaking his head.

"Que ha pasado? Por que corre usted?"

"What'd you tell him?" Joe Two-Fingers stepped

from behind the oak, his own rifle aimed at the Santanista's belly.

Kate answered, "He asked the Mexican what happened. Why he was running."

The small man was almost comical in his loosely fitting cotton uniform and bare feet. He gestured behind him. *"Muchos Texans, como las panteras salvajes, nos matan!"*

I translated for the other. "He said many Texans, like wild panthers, kill us."

"Who's he talking about?" Joe asked.

My hopes surged. Could it be . . . ? I remembered the cannonfire earlier. Suppressing the excitement boiling in my blood, I asked, *"¿Quien era su lider?"*

Without hesitation, he exclaimed, *"Santa Anna. Nostros sequimos anna de santa de general."*

"What now?" asked Joe.

Kate explained, her voice trembling with excitement. "Santa Anna. Santa Anna was his leader."

In the meantime, all I could do was gape at the small man who stood cowering before me, trembling, fearing his own death. With a short jerk of the muzzle of my long rifle, I gestured for the diminutive man to go.

His eyes widened in surprise.

I jerked the muzzle again, harder this time. "*¡Vaya!* Go!"

He glanced at the others, and then like a frightened

rabbit, splashed across the creek and raced across the prairie, heading for Mexico.

Kate laid her hand on my arm. "Bob."

I looked down at her.

"Do you think it's true? Do you think Houston and his army whipped Santa Anna?"

Two more fleeing Santanistas splashed across the creek a hundred yards north of us. I looked at Joe and Rides-With-Rain. Both wore grins as wide as the Brazos River. "You bet I do!" I shouted, impulsively grabbing Kate around the waist and swinging her around. "You bet I do."

Chapter Nineteen

Finding the location of the battle was simple. We just rode in the direction opposite that of the fleeing Mexican soldiers.

An hour later, we swam Buffalo Bayou and rode up on the plains of San Jacinto. My senses recoiled when I spotted the hundreds of bodies sprawled across the vast plain, bodies dressed in the gaudy blue and red of the cavalry, bodies dressed in the simple white cotton fatigues. We reined up, staring at the carnage before us.

None of us could say a word. All we could do was stare.

Suddenly, two horsemen skidded to halt in front of us. Pistols aimed, hammers cocked, they both scowled at us. "What are you doing here? Who are you folks?"

Before I could reply, a familiar voice cried out. "Bob! Bob Walker! Is that you?"

Beyond the two riders, a third approached, Robert McAnella, who had ridden to James Fannin with me and whom I'd sent back to Sam Houston with word of Fannin's surrender.

He rode between the two sentries. "They're okay, boys." He nodded to me. "You remember Bob Walker? Back at Gonzales, General Sam sent him and me after Fannin." He introduced the sentries. "This here is Ed Sims out of Bastrop, and this galoot is Paul Jenkins from down on the Lavaca River."

Their scowls vanished. Jenkins nodded to Kate and the others. "Looks like you folks have come a good piece."

I ignored his remark. "What happened here, Robert? We must've run into a hundred Santanistas heading for Mexico as fast as they could run."

All three men laughed. "They best keep running." Ed Sims laughed. "General Sam Houston done whipped the whole Mexican army right into the ground."

"The whole . . ." I looked at Robert in disbelief.

He removed his floppy hat and dragged his buckskin clad arm across his forehead. I couldn't help noticing the blood on the sleeve. "Yep. We caught them napping. Twenty minutes and it was over. And not thirty minutes ago, we found Santa Anna."

Robert motioned for us to follow. "Come on, Bob.

Bring your friends. General Sam will be tickled to see you. He asked about you two or three times after I got back. He sure hoped you wasn't hurt none."

I held up my hand to stop him. "First, I got to tell you, Robert. It's about Pleasant."

He flinched. His eyes grew cold, and his face hard. Our eyes met. I read the question in his and nodded. His shoulders slumped. "I told him he was crazy to run off like that." He hesitated and looked deep into my eyes. "You see, he wanted to fight, and he just didn't have enough faith in the general. That's all. He was really a good boy," Robert added.

"I know. It happened about a hundred miles southwest. He'd had a run-in with some Santanistas."

For several seconds, Robert sat motionless, staring across the prairie. Finally, he shook himself from his trance. "Well, he got his chance to fight. Come on, Bob. Let's us go see the general."

We rode across the sun-drenched battlefield toward a spreading oak, around which a large band of Texans clustered in its shadows. We dismounted, and Robert elbowed his way through the crowd, making a path for us. "Make way, boys. Let us through. Someone here for the general to see."

Curious faces, stained with dirt and blood looked around. Curious eyes followed us. Curious frowns wrinkled foreheads.

I jerked to a halt when I saw General Houston lying on the ground, leaning back against the rough bark of the oak. Someone, a doctor, I guessed, was bandaging the general's ankle.

Houston looked up at me. A broad smile split his rugged face, and he extended a large hand. "Good to see you, son." He shifted his huge frame, trying to find a comfortable position. "I'm mighty pleased you made it back in one piece." His eyes focused on Kate and the girls.

I introduced them. Kate and the girls curtsied just like polite society. Ned and Joe nodded to the general.

When I introduced Rides-With-Rain, Houston grinned. "The chief and I been friends for many years."

Rides-With-Rain grunted.

"Looks like you picked up quite a following after you left Fannin, son." He chuckled.

"Yes, sir. I wanted to get back here and fight with you, but I couldn't." I paused, then added. "But I reckon we did our own fair share of fighting along the way, General."

His face grew serious. His eyes studied each member of our mismatched group. A young woman, four girls, an ex-slave, a mountain man with an imaginary Windingo on his shoulder, an Indian chief, and me.

He cleared his throat. "You're what Texas is all about. You're what we fought for today. We fought for a republic, where every woman and man no matter what race or religion can be free." He took my hand again and squeezed it hard. "No, son. I'd say you did more than your fair share of fighting."

Kate squeezed my arm. I looked down into her beaming face. Behind her, the girls smiled brightly. I laid my hand on hers. "Let's go on to Liberty. You all can stay with us until we find your folks."

"And then?" Kate looked deep into my eyes.

I gulped. My throat was suddenly dry, my lips parched. All four girls were giggling. Rides-With-Rain and Joe Two-Fingers were both grinning like they'd been whopped upside the head with a lunatic stick.

I mustered my courage. "Well, I suppose I'll just ride back there and see if there's any land available on the river. What do you think?"

Her eyes danced. "I think that's a fine idea, Mr. Walker. A fine idea."